BAD ZODIAC RISING

A novel by Jacob Oritt

Illustrated by Quinton Watson

BAD ZODIAC RISING

Copyright © 2016 by Jacob Oritt

Artwork by Quinton Watson

ISBN: 978-0-578-17847-9

For my parents, Jeff and Kristi Oritt
Thank you for introducing me to the wide world of books

PROLOGUE: PHILOSOPHICAL MUSINGS

Everyone knows the age old question considering which came first, the chicken or the egg? This philosophical train of thought can be applied to any belief system as well, in the form of the question which came first, the divine being, or the mortal who believed in the divine being? Do our very beliefs breath life into those we place upon a godly pedestal? Or were they always there?

Most mortals, when confronted with this question, will hem and haw and give you an answer based upon opinion. A holy man of the old world would argue that of course the Creator came first, and He then created man so that we might give praise and glory unto Him. But ask a New Age believer and they might very well tell you that it is the power of our belief that gives birth to the various pantheons and factions of gods and goddesses that have ruled over this planet since time immemorial.

I am one of the only creatures on your plane of existence that can give you a factual answer. The gods have indeed been here, on Earth as well as their own various Realms, since the birth of this universe. Someone once said "It matters not if you believe in God, for He believes in you". Truer words have never been spoken.

My symbiotic name is Dog. I am the human vessel of an animal god whose spirit was ripped away and forced to wander this plane of existence when humans began to settle on what is now called China centuries ago. Dog, as a deity, is one of twelve animal spirits that form a pantheon known in this day and age as a Zodiac.

I understand this may all sound somewhat confusing, and to my chagrin I can't answer all of your questions right now. I can only hope that I will live long enough to explain everything in time. For now, you just have to understand that some gods, divine though we may be, are not immune to the petty squabbles of humanity. For the Chinese Zodiac is a part of that humanity, and have been for so long that the dividing line between human and deity has become...blurred.

Through my ability to glimpse beyond the veil and see a hint at what has yet to pass, I have come to understand some of the machinations of one I once called brother. Even now I can feel him getting closer, which means I must leave this safe house and find yet another, for he will not rest until I have sworn myself to his cause. And if I will not, then he will instead have me dead at his feet.

1

Neither option can I accept, and so I will flee, and continue desperately to try to contact the one other pantheon of gods that still take a hand in shaping this world in the hopes of finding allies. They are an ancient pantheon, a Zodiac like mine, with their own mortal heroes that walk the earth with a mantle of divine power upon their shoulders. In this day and age, the majority of the worshipers of this Zodiac reside in what is now called the United States.

I must find a way to contact these Americans before it's too late.

Before Dragon gets there first.

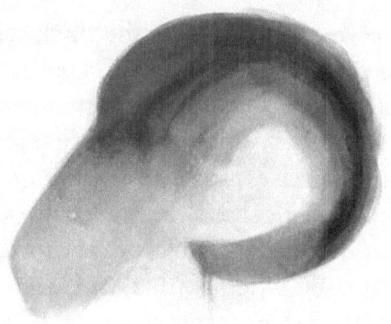

CHAPTER 1

ARIES

Aries is one of the most powerful signs in the zodiac. It is a sign representing war on both sides of the coin, the just and the jihad. It's a sign of reckless leadership and fearless control. So is it any surprise that the chosen Hero of Aries would be a woman?

9:43 PM PST, April 13, 2015

She sat perfectly motionless on the thick rug, one of only two decorations that her meditation room had. Her lynx familiar was in a state of hibernation in her lap, its furry, spotted chest rising and falling in time with her own. When she had first started using this space for her calming exercises, she had tried to go completely spartan and sit in the lotus position on the hardwood floor, but found that it was just not conducive to proper meditation, and she had nearly lost control. So when Karina, one of her fellow Zodiac Heroes, had bought her a shag carpet rug (red, of course, as suited her station), she had readily accepted it.

Madeleine, Hero of Aries, wore simple clothing over her slim but hard muscled body: cherry red leggings and a burgundy tank top. Her long wildfire-red hair was pulled back with a scarlet hair band. A few curly strands had escaped the confines of the band and drifted lazily in front of her face. They tickled now and then, but Maddy was so deep in her trance that she only acknowledged the desire to itch on the surface of her subconscious.

Besides the rug and her wildcat familiar, the room contained nothing beyond a single stand lamp in one corner that shed a stark illumination about the bare room. It had no windows to the outside world. No paintings had been hung up on the walls. It had absolutely nothing that could evoke any kind of an emotional response whatsoever.

She loved it.

Maddy had a special 'temple', as it were, to meditate in. It was no secret who the chosen Heroes were, and as such, they had followers. Maddy had collected a group of clingers-on over the years that called themselves her Watchers. They had built this temple for her out of cypress wood reinforced with steel up in the hills above her beloved San Francisco so that she would always have a quiet place to go when her seclusion was of great importance to the survival of the human race.

4

The temple consisted of two floors. The ground floor had three large bedrooms, two full bathrooms, a kitchen that was always kept stocked with a veritable cornucopia of food, and a living room packed wall to wall with movies and video games. Her Watchers spent shifts staying with her during her meditation month, and needed things to keep them busy.

The top floor was her meditation room. Nothing else. The only rule of the house was that her Watchers weren't allowed upstairs, and should she go nuclear, they were the ones who would get word to the other Zodiac Heroes as fast as possible. The Hero of Aries had been using this temple for three years now without incident.

Deep breathe in through the nose, focusing on the brightest shade of red that she could. Think of the first rays of sunlight pouring over the mountains, setting fire to the new day. This was her positive focus. This was her color that represented all the good in the world. This was her shade of peace.

Slow exhalation through the mouth, now imagining that her breath was a deep burgundy, a color halfway between wine and blood. This was her negative focus. This was her color representing all the bad in the world. This was her shade of war. This was her inner destruction, released as safely as possible.

Deep within her, at the center of her being, the power of War flowed through her veins like a roaring river of magma. The calm of her meditation was a protective shell she had built around herself. Safe within this shell, Maddy allowed her divine power to rage under her, around her, over her…but never through her. If her shell ever cracked…all was lost. Starting with her own humanity.

Eleven months out of the year, Maddy was a pillar of control. Part of her sign, her power, was control in of itself. But during the month of her sign, from late March to late April, her inner fire became a funeral pyre of wanton abandon. The divine mantle of power within her screamed out for battle, for death, for annihilation. Maddy had two options: enter solitary meditation for a month, or burn down the world.

She chose peace.

Others would have her choose differently.

While she meditated, Maddy cast her mind back to when she first met the others chosen by the Zodiac gods and goddesses to be

5

the standard bearers of power in the world. It was on her 18th birthday, when Aries herself had shown her the true measure of her power. And the inherent danger that lay within.

Up until that point she had known only a portion of the power of Aries. Due to the somewhat fragile state of the human body and mind before the 18th birthday, most of the gods and goddesses didn't allow a full connection to be made until that fateful day (except for Sagittarius, the only god who was well and truly out of his MIND; they all suspected that his chosen Hero was somewhat lacking of a full deck as well due to his god giving him full power access since the day he turned 13). The other divine beings allowed a minute connection that began at puberty to give the Hero plenty of time to become used to being something more than human.

The day Maddy turned 18 began like any other day. She awoke next to the yearling lynx kitten (named Spear) that was her familiar, a gift from Aries the year before. The wild kitty had a soul that carried a sliver of divinity, causing it to age at the same rate as a human, among other things. It was still small enough to hold in two hands.

The morning sun had just crested the horizon, sending out warm tendrils of light to begin the daily process of burning away the fog that enshrouded San Francisco each night like a cold blanket. Maddy climbed out of bed and stretched in the silent dawn, entwining her fingers and reaching up to the ceiling. Her back popped, loud as a gunshot in the quiet of the morning. Spear mimicked her, climbing to her over-large paws and stretching out like an accordion. It was adorable.

Next she snatched a polished mahogany brush (yet another gift from her divine benefactor) from the top of her dresser and padded over to the full length mirror in the corner of her bedroom, eyes still half shut and mind on the verge of falling back asleep. Maddy stepped up to the mirror, raising the brush automatically for the routine that would follow.

She looked up into what should have been her reflection and froze.

Eyes shot open wide as her eyebrows tried to climb straight up to the ceiling.

The brush, completely forgotten, dropped to the floor from a hand that had gone numb.

Aries was staring back at her out of the mirrored glass. The tall Amazonian goddess smiled and gave her a little wave. Maddy's mind fled all the way back to the land of dreams, leaving her body to slump down to the ground.

Lost within her memories, Maddy smiled. When she had awoken from her faint, it had been to find Aries rolling around on the carpet next to her, wrestling with Spear. Aries was giggling. Giggling. For some reason it had shocked Maddy right down to her core. Aries was the goddess of war! It was entirely inappropriate for a divine being to giggle.

Aries had taken the entire day to explain to Maddy what it meant to carry the full mantle of her power. The responsibility. The burden. She explained what she would deal with for an entire month every single year. Maddy learned that past Heroes hadn't handled the mantle too well. The last Hero of Aries who had lost control during his reigning month had touched off the Dark Ages. That was also the last time in history that a man had been allowed to carry the power of Aries. From that point forward, every Hero of War had been a woman.

In an attempt to end the day on a lighter note, Aries had shown Maddy a glimpse of her fellow Heroes. The goddess had turned Maddy's mirror into a looking glass and, one by one, introduced Maddy to the human pillars of the American Zodiac.

Two Pisces, both men and both thickly muscled, defined the division of Life and Death in the world.

One Taurus, male, large and solid, was a mountain of stability in a world that was ever changing.

Two Geminis, both women and as opposite in appearance as night and day. They were physical manifestations of Creativity and Logic, and wielded the power of gravity.

The afore-mentioned Sagittarius, tall and barrel-chested and entirely too male for his own good. His smile had carried a maniacal edge since his 13th birthday, when his god had 'blessed' him (or so he had said) with the full mantle of his power. He didn't blink much, but he was a powerful asset in a fight.

One Capricorn, female, with a dual ability to match her dual personality. She was the physical representation of the highs and lows that mankind struggled through every day. In previous generations, the Capricorn god had chosen two heroes to wield his duel ability, but then, there had never been a Hero like this one.

Maddy's reverie was cut off by the sound of something smashing downstairs. Slowly, carefully, she pulled herself up and out of her meditative state. A full thirty seconds passed before she felt in control enough to open her eyes and let the world back in.

The first thing she saw was Spear, now four years old and the size of a golden retriever, standing in front of the door that was shut but not locked (what lock in the world could stand up to her if she lost her mind?). Spear was growling softy and all of her fur was standing on end. Even the tufts of fur on her ears were quivering. Still fighting to keep the power flooding through her at bay, Maddy climbed to her feet and took a single step forward.

As if on cue, the door swung open silently on well oiled hinges, revealing two men standing in the shadows on the landing. There didn't seem to be anything extraordinary about them, but Spear immediately backed off, keeping her spotted body between Maddy and the strangers. Her growl had deepened in cadence, and that more than anything else put Maddy on alert. There was something…wrong about them.

One of the men stepped forward into the room, and Maddy immediately pegged him as the leader by body language alone. The stranger stood just shy of six feet, and moved languidly with a casual arrogance, acting for all the world as if he owned everything he laid eyes on. He was wearing a silver and black pinstripe suit that appeared molded to his body, complete with a black bowler hat. He had an immaculately trimmed beard which outlined a cruel mouth that seemed frozen in a permanent sneer. His nose was a jagged hook jutting out from the middle of his face, and his bright green eyes were set a little too close together. Everything about this man screamed 'predator'.

"'Ello, love," the man said quietly, with an accept that told her he was British and most likely born low class.

"Nice suit," Maddy fired right back. "Did you pull yourself out of the slums just last week?"

The Brit rocked back as if he had been slapped, but that sneer never left his face. "I wouldn't be so hasty with the insults, lass. Y'see, I know exactly who ye are. But I doubt you have any idea who *we* are, ye kennit?"

"I genuinely don't care. What have you done with my people?"

The sneer widened into a grin that never reached his reptilian eyes. "They're dead, lass. There's one more of us, and he's been having his merry time of it downstairs. Good sport, your people. Rat says they taste absolutely *delicious*."

"Rat?" Maddy's mind raced with preternatural speed to a conclusion that sent a shiver of apprehension running down her spine. "You're the Chinese Zodiac Heroes, aren't you?"

The 'Hero' tipped his hat. "Penny for the pretty lady. You may call me Dragon."

Maddy cocked an eyebrow, trying to maintain a cool composure as her inner power threatened to overwhelm her. "I don't know if you knew this, but you're not Chinese."

Dragon barked out a laugh. "Right observant you are! Y'see, the Chinese Zodiac operates a little differently from your American white bread Heroes. Way I understand it, here you lot are granted your abilities, or some such foolishness. The Chinese Zodiac Heroes take their divinity!"

The color drained from Maddy's face. "You kill for your power," she whispered.

"Yes'm."

"And you're here to try the same thing. You're going to try to take over our Zodiac."

Dragon tipped his hat once more. When he smiled, it was to expose teeth that were elongating, sharpening to razor points.

Maddy did the last thing the two killers were expecting: she threw her head back and roared out laughter, letting her power sweep away her control in a tidal wave. As she did, her clothes began to shimmer. The leggings she wore, starting at her ankles, shimmered straight out of existence, revealing legs that were wiry with corded muscle. At around the knees, her leggings melted and segmented together, hardening into a silvery organic-metallic chain mail battle skirt that seemed more liquid than solid.

Her laughter took on a physical edge, blasting out of her in a whirlwind that swirled around the room, forcing Dragon to clap a hand onto his hat to stop it from blowing away. As Maddy's leggings transformed up, so did her top transform down, starting at the shoulders. The organic metal chain mail spread down her torso and melded seamlessly into the skirt. The straps of the tank top flowed out and down over her arms, ending just above the wrists. Even her

9

hair tie transformed, spreading up and around her temples into an organic-metallic skull cap.

The second killer, nervous under his calm façade, took a step into the room, seemingly unfazed by the whirlwind. That single footstep shook the floorboards. Maddy, mid transformation, didn't notice. If she had opened her eyes, she would have seen that this second man was massive, nearly seven feet tall with skin as dark as onyx. He was a native Nigerian, and had ripped the power of Ox from the previous Hero only a year before. Despite his mass, he was still coming into his powers, and he was the least confident of the three would-be usurpers. The only reason he was there at all was that Dragon had no one else he could trust. The Chinese Zodiac Heroes weren't known for their teamwork. Paranoia went with the job.

The last thing to transform was her lynx familiar. Spear reared up on her hind legs, thinning and lengthening, taking on her true form: a living battle spear nearly seven feet long, tipped on either end with a spear point, and balanced at the top with a half-moon axe blade on one side and a wickedly curved spear point on the other.

The laughter died away, and for a moment silence reigned. Then Maddy opened her eyes, revealing two pits of bottomless fire. The demigoddess smiled. "Who dies first?" she whispered.

A giggle sounded from behind her, and she whipped around, leveling her battle spear at the short, nearly emaciated man that stepped up and out of the shadow that her lamp cast.

Rat.

Blood dripped down his unshaven chin and splattered on the floor. His eyes, one blue and one black, rolled madly in his head. Rat's fingers were tipped in claws that still had chunks of flesh speared on them. Even as Maddy watched, Rat lifted one hand to his mouth and nibbled on the meat, grinning away all the while.

Her rage grew to a burning inferno in a split second, and she was on the verge of truly letting her inner goddess loose and waving goodbye to her humanity forever...when two more people joined the fray, via smashing straight down through the roof. It was enough of a shock to push away her rage just for a moment, and Maddy wrestled her control back into her possession.

"Barin? Max? How the hell-" Maddy started to exclaim. The Chinese Heroes were frozen in place.

Max, one of the Pisces Heroes, spared a quick smile for her. "Hey, dear. Heard from one of your Watchers that you were in a spot of trouble. Karina got us here as fast as she could."

Dragon snarled, furious. "Gemini whore! Your Zodiac would dare interfere-"

"-with the attempted murder of our friend?" Max shot back sarcastically. "You bet your British ass we would."

Barin, the Hero of Taurus, stood a full head shorter than the Nigerian, and yet something about his presence made him seem twice as big. He turned to face the giant black man. "You're Ox, I suppose. Ivy Pulled in all the information she could about your Zodiac before Karina Pushed us up here. Way I hear it, you're an unstoppable force. Let's find out, shall we?"

Ox felt his nervousness dissipate with the thrill of the challenge, and he roared out his battle cry, leaping across the distance between them. He lowered his head and dropped a shoulder at the last instant, meaning to plow right through Barin. He hit the Taurus Hero mid-torso…and rebounded so hard he flew back out of the room, taking half of the doorway with him in an explosion of wood and screeching metal. Barin leapt after him, skin rippling, hardening.

Rat, seeing the odds turning against them, spun around and made to jump back through the shadow to safety. Max cried out "Oh no you don't!", reaching up to his forehead to yank his Deathmask down onto his face. Time slowed down as the dark power flowed through him, and he threw his body forward to tackle Rat. They both hit the shadow and disappeared. Maddy and Dragon were left alone.

Maddy, barely back in control, lowered her spear to point directly at Dragon's heart. "You want my power? Come and get it."

Dragon screamed out his rage, triggering his own transformation. Smoke streamed out of his nostrils as claws tore out of his fingertips and toes, ruining the expensive shoes he was wearing. Dragon's skin turned green and hardened into overlapping scales, while massive wings tore their way out of his spine, splattering his own blood across the walls. The walls smoked as his acidic blood began to eat through the wood and into the steel framework beneath. His irises shifted from round to almond and turned a sullen red. Liquid fire dripped out of the corners of Dragon's mouth and hissed as it hit the floor. He gained a foot in height as his muscles burst and reformed, bigger, stronger. Even his bones grew in density, adding to his strength. All of this happened in the space of a few heartbeats.

Maddy didn't even flinch.

Dragon, holding onto his own humanity by the thinnest of threads, roared in challenge and dove forward, claws outstretched as he sought to tear her limb from limb. Maddy spun her spear up in front of her in a defensive position, and Dragon's claws closed on the haft. With no hesitation, Maddy head butted him right in the center of his scaly forehead. Dragon's roar cut off as he rocked back in surprise more than pain.

"You think to challenge me, the Hero of war, in the middle of my month of power?!" Maddy screamed. She whipped the axe blade of her spear around in a tight circle, and one of Dragon's claws went spinning away in a spray of greenish blood. Dragon howled and dove at her again, ducking under the spear and catching her at the waist, driving the two of them through the back wall and out into the night.

They spun through the air slowly, almost gracefully. Dragon snapped his head forward, trying to get his razor teeth into her neck. Maddy got an armored elbow up and drove it into one of Dragon's eyes. It burst and Dragon screamed again, this time in pain as half of his world went black in an instant.

They crashed through one massive redwood tree, then another, neither of them giving any mind to the impact as they focused on the fight at hand. The ground rushed up to meet them, and they finally bounced apart, coming to a forcible halt in the middle of one of the many herb gardens that the Watcher's cultivated around Maddy's temple.

Dragon was back up in an instant to press his attack , despite the remains of one eye dribbling down his cheek. Maddy, still on the ground, swept a leg out and caught Dragon in the right kneecap, which let go with an audible POP! Dragon went down howling, spewing fire all around them, burning her herb garden to ash.

"You think that power stolen is greater than power granted?" Maddy shouted as she climbed back up to her feet. Her voice echoed around the burning garden. "You are nothing more than a petty thief. You have done *nothing* to earn your power! I was born into my place, and have earned the right to it time and time again!" She drove a spear point into one of Dragon's wings as he writhed around on the ground, pinning him like a bug. He tried to pull it free and only succeeded in shredding it further, evoking a fresh set of screams.

"You think to take my power from me?! *My power would burn you to ash where you lie!* **You don't know the true meaning of war!**" Maddy pulled the spear free and rammed it down through his other wing. The ground beneath him was bubbling, smoking as his acidic blood spilled out.

"Please…" he whispered, helpless beneath her.

Maddy's lips peeled back from her teeth in a feral snarl. She yanked her spear back one last time and drove it straight through his throat. Dragon couldn't even pull breath in through his mangled windpipe to allow him a final scream; all that came out was a wet gurgle. His one working eye rolled into the back of his head as he passed out from the pain. Moments later, death mercifully claimed him.

As his human spirit passed on, a living shadow tore itself free of his body. Maddy only got a single glimpse before it whirled around and flew off into the night. It looked like the shadow of a massive dragon.

Maddy held her spear above her head and howled her challenge of war to the whole world. Her mind was consumed with thoughts of death and destruction. No one could stand before her! No one would dare! She would wrap this world in chains of fire and burn everything to cinders! She would-

Something massive barreled into her, knocking her to the ground. She looked up in time to see a centaur shrinking back down into the body of a man who looked vaguely familiar to her, but no coherent thought could penetrate through the bubbling miasma that was her mind. All she saw was another being trying to subjugate her, take what was hers-

"Maddy!" the man shouted down at her, and she felt something human stirring within her madness… "Maddy, I know you're in there! Listen to me! LOOK AT ME! I can help you! I can take this madness away from you but you have to look! AT! *ME!*"

The last word drove itself through her, past the maelstrom in her mind, and she locked her gaze on his. His irises were shifting, spinning around so fast she felt herself being drawn in…

Max and Barin walked slowly into the clearing, drawn by the screams they had heard only moments before. Both were on edge; they knew exactly what it would mean if Maddy lost complete

13

control. Max still had his Deathmask on, was filled to bursting with his dark power. Barin had his fists clenched so tightly he could feel his stone transformation starting to spread up through his forearms; it was only by sheer force of will that he didn't complete the transformation on the spot. He never transformed completely unless it was utterly necessary. Besides, he'd already transformed once tonight and he was exhausted.

They saw Maddy lying on the ground in full battle regalia. Her spear was lying near one outstretched hand, shimmering slowly back into lynx form. They saw Peter, their friend and fellow Hero, of the mad god Sagittarius. He was kneeling on her chest, pinning her to the ground. They both had their teeth clenched, hers in rage and his in pain. They saw an inky black substance writhing up from her flaming gaze, and as they looked on, they saw that blackness drive itself straight into Peter's eyes. His mouth opened in a soundless scream as he pulled her madness into himself, joining it to his own.

Max made a move to intervene, but Barin grabbed him. "This has to happen."

"It could kill him!" Max shouted, trying in vain to pull away from the unyielding grip of Taurus.

"Better him than the world," Barin said softly.

For what seemed an infinite moment in time the madness of an unleashed Aries poured straight into the unbalanced soul of Sagittarius, the only Hero to be given full power when he was still basically a child. The only Hero who had been driven at least partially mad by his power. The only one of them who could balance her madness with his own and, hopefully, save them both. Save them all.

The last of Maddy's darkness rocketed out of her and into Peter. His body was thrown backwards a dozen feet by the sheer force of it. She immediately went limp, battle regalia automatically shifting back to her meditation clothes. Spear, back in lynx form, curled up next to her and mewed piteously.

Max went straight to Maddy, tearing his Deathmask off as he went. He reached down to check her pulse. Low, but steady. He breathed a sigh of relief, and then looked around to see Barin checking Peter. "He ok?"

Barin looked up, gaze troubled. "He has a pulse. Doesn't look hurt. He's...laughing."

"He's *what?*!"

Barin stood up, brushing himself off. "You remember how he was before? After he got his full power when he was 13? How it changed him? And now this? He might not come back from this. Hell, he might not even understand what it was he did-"

"Worth it."

Max and Barin both jumped a foot in the air. Barin whirled around to see Peter on his feet, wobbling slightly. His eyes were a little too wide, but his gaze was steady. His mouth twitched at one corner as if a laugh was trying to force itself out. He gulped and glanced at Maddy. "How is she?"

"She'll be fine..." Max said slowly.

Peter nodded, eyes wide, hands clenched tightly into fists at his side. He could feel his fingernails biting through the skin of his palms, and he focused on the pain. "What happened to you guys?"

The two Heroes looked at each other. Barin stepped forward.

"I tangled with Ox, got him on the ropes, let him go. He was scared. I don't think he's ever met his match before."

"Barin, he's a killer!" Max ground out, trying to reign in his emotions.

Barin looked at his friend calmly. "But I'm not. What about you? What happened with Rat?"

Max shook his head angrily. "The little bastard got away. He was like an eel, always twisting away and trying to run from the fight. He didn't get away clean, though. I got in a lucky hit and shattered his jaw just before he gave me the slip. He's gonna be eating through a straw for a while."

"Good," Peter said firmly. Lord, but his eyes were so wide. Barin didn't think he'd blinked since he'd seen him get up. "Then let's get Maddy back into her house and call another cell of Watchers. They can clean up the bodies and get the house back in working order."

Max stared, incredulous. "After everything she just went through, that's all you can say?"

"It's still her month. I've taken this round of unleashed rage from her, but that doesn't mean she's not a danger anymore. She still needs to meditate her way through until the next sign, that's you Barin, comes into power. After that...well, then we'll see what can be done."

Nothing more needed to be said. Barin went over to Maddy and picked her up as easily as if she were a child. Spear allowed him to carry her mistress, but stayed right on his heels as he walked back towards the house. Max moved to follow, but noticed he was the only one. He turned…and Peter was gone.

Be well, my brother, Max sent out after his departed friend. *I worry that we'll have need of you in the days to come. Something tells me this attack by the Chinese Zodiac is only the beginning…*

4/14/15

Yesterday I took a life. No, let me rephrase that. I killed someone. Murdered him. I don't care that he was a bad guy. I don't care that I have the spirit of war inside of me. I don't even care that it was in self defense, which is all the other Heroes can say to try and freaking reassure me. I killed someone, and now I have to live with that for the rest of my life!

I know that I had lost control and that it was my power, and not ME, in the drivers seat. That just makes it that much scarier! What if Peter hadn't shown up to take away my madness? Looking back on what happened, I remember exactly how it felt to want to burn the world down. What the hell kind of power is this, that would make me want that?

After Peter vanished to the gods know where, Max and Barin stuck around and talked me through it. They waited with me until a new cell of watchers arrived to start cleaning up and to put my temple back together.

Temple. HA! Temples are for gods. I'm just a girl with a nuclear bomb inside of her, and last night that bomb almost went off. Max kept reminding me that what I really did was stop the Chinese Zodiac from... I don't even know what they were here to do! Dragon supposedly wanted to kill me and steal my power, but can they do that? What if Dragon HAD killed me? I think it's far more likely that my power would have gone straight back to Aries, and maybe it should have! The other Heroes, they all have beneficial powers, or at least that's how it seems. Don't know so much about Peter, although he IS the one who saved me. But the power of Aries? The power of war? There is only one thing that my ability can be used for. Destruction. Maybe the world would be better off without a 'Hero' of Aries.

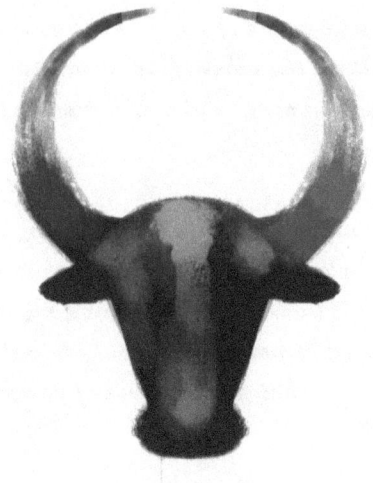

CHAPTER 2

TAURUS

Taurus is the sign of the centered and settled. Taurus is the rock that weathers the storm. Taurus is not quick to anger or fits of passion; Taurus simply is.

8:00 PM PST, May 4, 2015

When the doorbell rang, Barin climbed slowly to his feet. The Hero of Taurus was tall and broad, with skin the color of burnished gold due to his Pakistani heritage. His short hair and serious eyes were a shade of brown so dark they were nearly black, and the same would have gone for his beard, had he ever decided to grow one out. But it was a matter of pride for him that he always kept himself perfectly clean shaven and with a short, no-nonsense haircut. He liked to present a serious face to the world, as befitted one of his station.

Barin walked with a steady gait to the solid oak door, grasped the knob in a firm grip with his large hand, and pulled the door open. It wasn't that Barin was deliberately trying to make the person on the other side wait for him, it was simply that he didn't do anything rushed.

Except for that fight a few weeks ago...

Barin shook his head, dispelling that line of thought like it was so much smoke. "Hi Karina. Come on in."

"Thanks!" she said with her trademark smile. The sight of it brought a grin to his own face as if by magic. There was something ineffable about the Gemini Heroes that made people happy.

Karina settled down in one of his well-worn leather armchairs, energy bubbling out of her. Her very presence made his apartment brighter. Literally. Barin's lamps shined like miniature suns whenever she came around.

Rather than sit down and get right to the point, Barin first offered her food and drink. Proper etiquette must always be observed. It's what separated them from the savages and the hasty people.

Karina declined food, but gladly accepted a bottled micro brew. After popping the tops off of two of them with his thumbs, momentarily turning them to stone so as not to cut himself, Barin handed one to his teammate and then sat down in a chair across from her.

Even then, Barin waited for her to take a sip before he began. "Thank you again for your help last month when Maddy was attacked at her meditation temple. Without you-"

"Hey, none of that," Karina cut in, waving her hand as if to physically brush off the possibility of something having gone wrong. "We're a team. This is what we do."

Barin nodded gratefully. "Regardless, thank you. Like I mentioned on the phone earlier, I wanted to get together with you and put our heads together on the bigger picture. I don't think this is the last we are going to see of the Chinese Zodiac Heroes."

Karina's smile slipped away as the mood sobered. The various lamps in the corners of the living room dimmed slightly with her mood. "I completely agree with you. And as much as I love the rest of our team, I think that you and I are best suited to do the recon work on this one."

"To be honest with you, I half expected you to bring Ivy along to our meeting tonight. I didn't think you two did much apart."

Karina chuckled. "Normally you'd be right. But she's been doctoring Crazy Pete, helping to keep his madness in check by regularly Pulling his sanity to the forefront of his mind."

"Using her abilities?"

"Mostly her feminine abilities, I think," she replied with a wink.

Barin nearly sprayed a mouthful of beer at his friend. "Gemini and Sagittarius? But after last month, he's even crazier than before!"

"Aren't we all? And if this attack by the Chinese Zodiac was the first of many, what better time for romance? When you don't know how long the world is going to last, you don't hold anything back."

Barin took a long moment to mull that over. At last he nodded. "Ok, I can see that. And Peter is a good guy, when you get past the psychosis and the neuroses." He shook his head. "This is all beside the point. What I was hoping we could do tonight is-"

"-use my power to try and pinpoint the entire Chinese Zodiac, and, if necessary, get warnings to rest of our team, who currently happen to be scattered across the states?"

Barin smiled. "Right. And I can help-"

"- keep me grounded, just in case someone in the Chinese Zodiac sees this coming and tries a mental attack while I'm outside of my body?"

"Gods, you're good."

Karina laughed. "Us Gemini Twins always did know more than we let on. And speaking of, I've already Pushed out and located the rest of our team, though I haven't sent a general warning to everyone. Yet."

The Hero of Taurus cocked an eyebrow. "Where is everyone? Not outside of calling range, I hope?"

"Depends on your definition of 'calling range'. Thankfully, most of us are within driving distance, here in Northern California." Karina held up her hands and started ticking off fingers as she named Heroes. "That includes you, me, Ivy, Peter, Maddy, and Sally right here in San Francisco. Oh, and Andy, the Leo Hero, lives here, too. I always forget about him, seeing as he almost never comes out with us. Aquarius, who I don't know if you've already met or not, is in New York City. The two Pisces boys are in Salt Lake City, Utah. Virgo is in Wyoming; Jackson Hole I think. One of the Cancer men is in Chicago, and the other is in New Orleans, but due to their abilities they could be here in a heartbeat."

"That just leaves, what, Libra and Scorpio, right? Where are they?"

"*They* are a huge pain in the ass to track down. Imani, the Hero of Scorpio, recently came into her powers, and wanted to celebrate with a major road trip across the Southern states. Brock, the Hero of Libra, has taken it upon himself to mentor her through the initial rush of becoming a demigoddess, and as such hit the road with her. It's hard to get a fix on them. Let's just hope that in a crisis, I could nail them down in time to get them suited up with the rest of us."

Karina finished her beer, and Barin immediately chugged his down and got up to grab them two more. She thanked him, they clinked bottles, and dove right back in.

"What I'm hearing is that we're spread out, but could mobilize fairly quickly if necessary," he mused.

"Most of us, at the very least." Karina agreed.

Barin took a deep breath. "Alright then. How do you want to get started with the Chinese Zodiac recon?"

She set her beer down on a hand-carved wooden coaster and stretched, popping her back. It sounded like firecrackers shooting up her spine. "Last month you, Max, and Maddy took on three of them. Dragon, Ox, and Rat, right? And Maddy killed Dragon?"

He nodded.

"Tell me again what happened when Dragon died."

Barin retold the story of how an inky black dragon-shaped shadow had torn itself free of the Brit's body and vanished. When he finished, Karina shivered, but her expression tightened with resolve.

"I was going to say we should start there, but on second thought that sounds scary as hell. Let's start with Ox. Since you fought him, I can use your experience to strengthen my connection to him when I Push."

She reached across the coffee table towards him, palms up. Barin set down his beer and took them, dwarfing hers with his own large hands. He tightened his fingers, and opened himself up to his transformation. Barin's golden-hued skin darkened slightly as it hardened into organic stone. Karina's hands, physically linked to his transformation, began to harden as well. But what shocked her the most was the feeling of her mind hardening, strengthening. It felt like her inner resolve was being banded in iron.

Karina gasped as she felt her entire aura become surrounded in a protective shell.

"Are you alright?" Barin exclaimed, uncertainty threaded through his tone.

"I'm fine," she assured him. "It's just a little...disorienting at first." She took a few deep breaths to steady herself. "Alright then, here we go..."

Karina Pushed her mind outside of her body, holding on tight to that connection with her teammate. Now freed from the limitations of her physical body, she had a complete 360 degree awareness of the world around her. It wasn't sight, although that's the closest connection that her mind made to what she was feeling. It was like she had awoken new senses that could never be defined by the limits of the human body.

Karina Pushed harder and left Barin's apartment behind, soaring up into the night sky above San Francisco. Orienting on the feeling of Ox that she got from Barin's mind, she sent herself rocketing away over the ocean.

Barin, normally a font of harmony and patience in this chaotic world, suddenly found himself fraught with uncertainty and nervousness. He tried constantly to push himself into Karina's thoughts, to see what she was seeing, if only to reassure himself that she was ok, but he was rebuffed every time by the shield wall that he himself had put around her. It quickly became worrying.

Not too much time passed, however, before her eyes shot open.

"Two for one!" Karina exclaimed before Barin even had a chance to react to the fact that she was back and she was ok. "I found Ox on the outskirts of London of all places, and he was with Tiger! And it gets even crazier. By Pushing into Ox's mind, just for a second, I got a complete readout of Ox, Rat, Tiger, Rabbit, and Snake before he felt me wandering around in there and I had to beat feet! Well, not physical feet, but you know what I mean. Anyway, I'm actually pretty sure they're the only ones involved from the Chinese Zodiac. You're never going to believe who Tiger is!"

Barin cocked his head, smiling at the huge outburst. "Who?"

"Dragon's freaking older brother! That's how they're involved in the Chinese Zodiac! Tiger is ex-military, and super duper scary by the way, and the two brothers hunted down the old Tiger and Dragon Heroes and respectively murdered them so they could each get a power and then watch each others back!"

Barin shook his head for what felt like the hundredth time tonight, trying to process all of this new information and put the pieces together. "So who's idea was it for them to come after us?"

"Don't know that one yet. I just know that Tiger is beyond pissed. Not sad, not grieving, just furious that we were even *able* to kill his little brother!"

"Ok, good to know. What about Rabbit and Snake?"

"French and Indian, respectively. I'll tell you more about them later. Right now I'm on a roll! Time to figure out what happened to the Dragon shadow while I still have an open connection to their group."

An electric shiver worked its way down Barin's spine at her bravado. "Are you sure?"

Karina looked at him, expression turning serious. "Yes. We need to know this. We're fighting blind without this info."

"Alright then. Ready when you are."

Karina closed her eyes and Pushed out of her body once more.

Minutes passed. Those minutes became an hour. Barin felt his worry spiking higher and higher as the time slipped by him. To calm himself, he entered a meditative state of mind, slowing his breathing, all the while feeding more and more of his energy into the protective shell that surrounded Karina's mind.

Suddenly Karina was back, eyes open wide, sweat beading on her forehead, yanking her hands away from him and breaking the connection. She was panting as if she had just sprinted for a mile straight.

"Oh gods...Barin...I was wrong...it's not just...a couple of them...it's all of them...and *he's* leading them..."

Barin's adrenaline peaked in an instant, skin beginning to harden in automatic response to the threat that he suddenly felt pressing in from all around him.

"Who? Who is leading them? What did you see?"

"It's Dragon..."

"What, a new Dragon Hero already?"

She shook her head wildly, black hair flying chaotically around her face. "The Dragon god himself is here."

Barin's jaw dropped wide open. "Oh my gods. We have to warn-"

His front door crashed open, flying off of its hinges and punching a hole through his living room wall and into the kitchen beyond. A tall wiry man with an unkempt mop of bright silver hair stood in the open doorway balanced on one foot, his other foot extended in front of him. He smiled, and the temperature seemed to drop ten degrees. His smile transformed his face into the face of death.

"*Bonjour*," he said jovially in a light tenor voice, acting for all the world as if he had just arrived to a dinner party. "I am *Monsieur* Rabbit. I am here to kill you, yes? *Je prefere* before *mon frère* Snake arrives *avec optimisme.*"

Rabbit bounded into the room, leaping straight for Karina. She Pushed herself up into the air, allowing him to pass harmlessly beneath her.

The Chinese Zodiac Hero laughed, positively delighted that he had missed. "A challenge! *Oui!*" He rebounded off the wall and

24

leaped higher, plowing into Karina from behind. They smashed through Barin's aspen coffee table and landed in a tangle of arms and legs and slivers of wood. Rabbit was back up in the blink of an eye, rearing a leg back before driving one of his feet into Karina's side. She gasped out as she felt several ribs crack.

All of this happened in an instant, while Barin was still forming a single thought: *He's too fast.* Then he saw Rabbit kick Karina, and coherent thought came to a grinding halt.

Barin's body, already in mid-transformation, turned completely to organic stone even as Rabbit was pulling his leg back for another kick.

"Karina!" Barin roared out. "PUSH!"

Karina reacted without thinking, Pushing at Rabbit with all of her strength. Rabbit was hit with the equivalent force of a bottled hurricane and thrown off his feet.

Directly at the Hero of Taurus.

Barin's fist connected solidly, and suddenly Rabbit wasn't in his apartment anymore. Whether he was even still alive was up for debate.

Barin let go of his stone form immediately as he rushed over to Karina's side. By the time he knelt down, he was completely human again.

"Are you ok?"

The tenderness in his voice helped Karina push through the pain that was wracking her body. "I think so. A few cracked ribs. And the beginning of a major migraine. I haven't hit anyone with a Push that hard *ever*."

Barin smiled. "You should have seen the look on his face right before I hit-"

"Barin!" Karina screamed out.

Barin felt needles stab into his neck. There was pain...and then there was nothing.

The first thing he heard as consciousness began to swim back into his mind was crying.

Who's crying?

He thought he heard words intermixed with the crying, but couldn't make them out. He wanted to concentrate harder, but he was just so tired.

Did someone get hurt? Why do I hear crying?

Pause.

Why can't I move?

With a herculean effort, he forced his eyelids apart. They felt as if they weighed a hundred pounds. Each.

As his eyes opened, he began to understand what the voice was saying.

"Please come back, Barin...I need you...please don't leave..."

"Karina?" he croaked out.

"Barin?! Oh thank the gods!"

Arms went around him and squeezed, bringing a groan of pain to his lips.

"Easy there, I'm fragile."

Karina half laughed/half sobbed. "You? The Hero of Taurus is fragile?" But she let up a bit.

"What happened? I thought we won, and then everything went black."

Karina laughed again, and explained to Barin what had transpired while he had been unconscious.

Apparently Rabbit had been a distraction. While the two of them were caught up fighting the vicious Frenchman, an Indian man ("Snake", she said) had snuck in the back. As soon as Barin had turned from stone back to human, Snake had slithered up from behind and bitten him in the neck. He hadn't even stuck around to make sure the bite had done the job. Either he was that arrogant, or that afraid to have to face them directly if it didn't work.

"I think they're still trying to figure out our powers just as much as we're trying to figure out theirs. The Chinese Zodiac is obviously already on high alert since we managed to kill their Dragon Hero in the first attack. And now the Dragon god himself is here, and let me tell you, he's absolutely terrifying. I can only imagine what kind of fear he's instilled in them." Karina swiped a hand across her eyes, wiping away her tears and smearing mascara across one cheek.

Barin's brain was still fuzzy, and it was taking him time to sort through everything Karina was saying. "So how did you save me?"

"I don't think I could have if Snake had stuck around and pushed his advantage. The poison in his bite is lethally toxic; I felt it as I Pushed it out of your neck. As soon as I was fairly certain I had gotten it all, I wrapped a bandage around the wound and held pressure on it. I remembered you had mentioned once that your body reacts instinctively to wounds, closing up and hardening to

26

prevent blood loss. Sure enough, only a minute or two passed before the puncture wounds sealed right up."

Barin smiled up at her. "You saved my life. I'm going to buy you so many bottles of wine."

She laughed long and hard at that, and it only sounded a *little* forced. "You're making jokes already. I think that means it's safe to say the danger has passed."

Barin sobered up instantly, smile falling right off of his face. "The danger is just beginning. It's time to call in the others."

5/5/15

I almost died. I keep thinking that I should be more scared that I am, but the truth is, all I feel is this burning ember of warmth inside of my chest. I close my eyes and all I see is Karina's face. Her smile. The way her black hair cascades down her back like a river of silk. I want to run my fingers through that hair.

I really should be focused on the task at hand! I know that. The intel that Karina gathered about the Chinese Zodiac is invaluable, and we can hopefully use it to get a jump start on this burgeoning war, maybe even take the fight to them instead of waiting in fear for their next attack. Because as Karina learned, there WILL be a next attack. They aren't done yet, not by a long shot.

But it's like Karina said when she was talking about how her Twin and Sagittarius have been getting closer. In these times of war and strife, when the butcher has yet to finish tallying his bill, what better time for love? No holding back. No regrets.

I think I'll pay Karina a visit, and maybe bring along a bottle of wine. I did promise to buy her wine in thanks for saving my life, right?
Here's hoping the world keeps spinning long enough for me to ask her out.

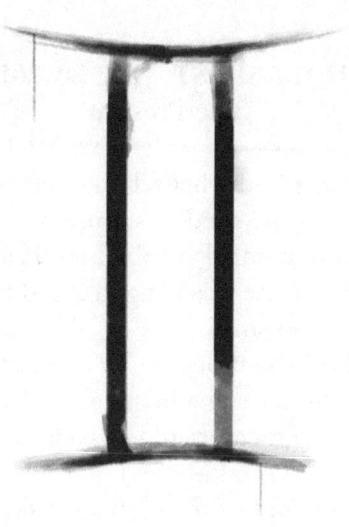

CHAPTER 3

GEMINI

Gemini is the sign of the twins, simultaneously opposite and identical. They are the artist and the scientist, the dreamer and the builder, and together they represent the primordial force of gravity in every way, shape, and form.

11:11 AM PST, June 20, 2015
The Present

Ivy woke up in a body that felt like one gigantic bruise. Her eyelids fluttered open as she tried to suppress a groan and failed.

As she began to mentally probe herself for more serious injuries, she realized that she was lying in a bed that wasn't hers. First of all, it's several sizes too small.

It's a hospital bed, she thought. *I'm in a hospital.*

The reason why she's in a hospital eluded her. *But that's alright,* she thought. The memory didn't seem too important at the moment.

Panic struck her out of the clear blue sky, panic that she didn't understand. What she *did* understand, however, is that there should be someone with her. Maybe more than one, but at least one for certain. Her head whipped back and forth, auburn hair flying about almost of its own volition as she searched about the room she's in, without consciously realizing who she was looking for.

As disoriented as she was, it took her a minute before she came to the conclusion that she wasn't alone in her hospital room. Lying in a hospital bed of his own opposite her is a shaggy bearded man that looked to be about her age. His eyes were closed, and his face had been beaten so badly that it takes a little scrutiny to recognize-

PETER!

And it all came flooding back.

The trip that she had been certain was doomed from the start.

The terror.

The rage.

The flight.

Ivy felt her consciousness swimming away from her. She's out before her head hits the pillow.

6:30 PM PST, June 5, 2015
The Recent Past

"It's been a month!" Peter was pacing back in forth in front of the Gemini Twins. He'd been pacing like that for the better part of an hour. In one of his saner moments earlier, he'd admitted that constant movement helped him keep a grip on himself.

Although Ivy and Karina were the chosen Heroes of Gemini and as such were known as the Twins, that term couldn't be farther from the truth. To start with, they weren't even the same age, let alone the same ethnicity. Both women were petite, but it was there that the similarities ended.

Ivy was 29-almost-30, with long, wild hair that looked light brown or dark red depending on the way light bounced off of it. Her green eyes each contained a single mysterious freckle in the iris, and she had the kind of fair complexion that's always attributed to either vampires or the Irish. Ivy was the latter. She was also drop-dead gorgeous, short and slender yet curvy in all the right places, and in a different lifetime where she wasn't hand selected to be a demigoddess, Ivy easily could have been a famous actress or rock star. If Helen of Troy had the face that launched a thousand ships and started a war, Ivy had the sensuality that would have brought every one of those ships back with a single wry twist of her lips. Paris would have walked right over Helen to get to Ivy faster.

Karina was just-turned-32, from Argentina, with long black hair that shimmered like the finest silk and blue eyes that sparkled like diamonds. Karina had the kind of curvaceous beauty that would have inspired the poets of old to write endless ballads about her, while they simultaneously fought over her favor and attention. Her smile was the kind that melted hearts and set passions aflame, for she smiled with her entire soul.

Together they shared the ability to manipulate gravity, Karina being the Pusher and Ivy being the Puller. Their power was in no way limited to physical objects, although the physical realm was the one in which they exercised their power most frequently.

Ivy Pulled Peter's attention to her to get him to stop pacing and griping for a moment.

"We can't expect the other Heroes to drop everything and come on this mission with us. They have very understandable concerns about this whole thing. Not to mention, most of them

31

haven't *personally* seen what we are up against. And you know what they say: seeing is believing."

"Tell that to Barin," Karina muttered.

The look that Ivy turned on her Twin was sympathetic but firm. "Karina, just because we carry divine power doesn't make us divine beings. We're all still human. We can't *force* the others to come with us."

Karina bounded to her feet, eyes blazing. "Why the hell not?!"

"Because then we would be the bad guys."

That brought Karina up short. She closed her eyes and sucked in a deep breath, reminding herself not to take out her fury on her teammates.

Peter took the opportunity to fill the silence. "It is what it is," he announced. "so if we're going to go, let's go already."

11:18 AM PST, June 20, 2015
The Present

Ivy tossed and turned in her hospital bed, lost in memories that were flooding through her dreaming mind. The heart rate monitor near her began to let out a shrill alarm as adrenaline spiked through her body.

6:45 PM PST, June 5, 2015
The Recent Past

The three Heroes stood in a circle on Karina's front lawn, hands linked tightly.

"Remember," Karina said. "I'm Pushing us over an entire ocean. I've never tried something this extreme before, and I've never *physically* been to our actual landing zone. I'm going completely from psychic memory here, from when I mind-jumped to England to find the Chinese Zodiac group and stumbled on a warehouse that several of them were hiding out in, including Snake."

"Wait a minute," Peter interrupted, eyes a little too wide. "are we all forgetting about the fact that the Dragon god himself is on our plane of existence?! Going on a potentially suicidal mission to

32

attempt to save our friend's life, I get that. I jive with that pretty well, actually. But if we run into the Dragon god without more firepower, we're toast!"

Karina was shaking her head before Peter had stopped talking. "I'm 99% positive that the Dragon god can't interfere with us, at least not yet. When I mentally probed them last month, I felt that his power was...withdrawn somehow. Yes, he's in our realm, but he still needs the other Chinese Zodiac Heroes to carry out his will."

"I sincerely hope you're right. Either way, that's all the concerns I have at the moment." Peter shut right up, trying his hardest to look calm and nonchalant about the whole thing, despite the fact that his heart was racing like a jackhammer and his throat was as dry as a desert.

"Anyway, " Karina resumed. "the plan is to hit the ground running, literally. We go in, find Snake, force him to give us an antidote for the poison he injected into Barin."

Peter let go of Karina's hand, on his left, and raised it like a child in school. "I have another concern."

Karina ground her teeth while Ivy tried, unsuccessfully, to suppress a small smile.

"What if there's no antidote to Snake's venom? Secondly, I thought you'd managed to Push all of the poison out of his system? Ergo...um...what's the point of this mission again?"

Karina's eyes burned with a silvery light as her power flooded through her system. "I *thought* I'd gotten all of the poison out of him, but then last week he collapsed for no reason and was rushed to the hospital and put on life support. OBVIOUSLY I missed some of the poison and it just now got through his inner biological defenses. Dammit Peter, I explained all of this earlier!"

Peter blinked rapidly a few times and shook his head. "Sorry. Get a little confused sometimes. So then, back to my question about the possibility of there not being an antidote to Snake's venom? Unless you explained that before, too..." The mentally unstable demigod squeezed his eyes shut, trying to reorganize his thoughts and memories.

Karina raised her chin and stared up at her infuriating teammate. "If we can't save Barin, then we'll do the next best thing. Get vengeance."

11:22 AM PST, June 20, 2015
The Present

"Doctor, we're losing her!"

"I need a crash cart over here, now!"

Ivy's body thrashed violently as medical personnel swarmed around her, trying desperately to keep her alive.

7:00 PM PST, June 5, 2015
The Recent Past

The three Heroes made the trip over the ocean in silence, with Karina maintaining a constant Push on the continent they were leaving behind them and Ivy Pulling on their group to ensure they didn't get separated. The only sound was the wind rushing past them at near supersonic speeds.

They should have frozen into popsicles within the first five minutes of the journey. However, a side effect of Ivy's Pull on the group was that she managed to maintain a Pull on their body heat as well, allowing very little of it to escape into the upper atmosphere. Regardless, they approached the island of Great Britain with teeth chattering and appendages slightly blue.

As they began to drop down out of the sky toward a dark warehouse in a shabby and poorly lit part of the country, Karina lessened her Push on the now distant North America and began a secondary Push on the ground rushing up to meet them. It wouldn't do to kill their team before they even got a chance to fight.

The warehouse grew bigger and bigger before them, revealing details. Most of the windows had been broken and now gaped at them like the maw of a beast with poor dental hygiene. The west wall was covered in phosphorescent graffiti and cast an eerie glow on the trash-littered parking lot that stood empty except for the burned out husks of a handful of compact cars. A massive shattered skylight with only a few remaining shards of glass clinging to it was visible in the middle of the roof, and Ivy Pulled them all towards it, like iron to a lodestone. They dropped through silently, and, with a final Push against the ground from Karina, landed as soft as a trio of feathers.

Time stopped, and several things happened at once.

Snake shot up out of the ground at Ivy's feet and bit into her neck.

Rat materialized from a shadow behind Karina and put a small handgun to the back of her head.

A voice heavily laced with a Russian accent boomed out from the back of the warehouse. "No one moves."

Peter ignored the voices in his head screaming out for action and obeyed the Russian. His wide eyes were locked on Ivy's. There was no fear in her steady gaze, in spite of the fact that imminent death was currently piercing her neck. Only fury at being caught unaware.

Karina was shaking, and looked about ready to launch an all out attack regardless of the level of danger surrounding them. Her eyes darted wildly around the warehouse, searching for the leader. For there was no mistaking the tone of command in the Russian voice. Had they found Dragon's replacement Hero?

Not one but two men stepped out of the shadows clinging to the rear of the warehouse. The one on the left was stocky and dressed in laborer's clothes, faded jeans and a dark flannel work shirt, both of which were covered in stains that Karina could only hope was oil and grime. The one on the right was much bigger, at first glance looking to be close to six and a half feet tall, and fully decked out in military fatigues, with camouflage paint covering every inch of exposed skin. It looked natural, as if he never took it off.

Karina contemplated Pushing them both through the back wall and not letting up until they were in the middle of the ocean.

The laborer smiled as if he had heard her thoughts. "You will be thinking of killing us, yes?" He chuckled. His Russian accent made him sound like a bad James Bond villain. "That is of course your decision. But know that if you do, you will die. Your friend with the man at her throat, she will die. And your bodyguard, he will fight to the death, but he will die in the end. And your trip will have been for nothing."

Karina ground her teeth, but didn't respond. She also didn't kill them.

Ivy did the one thing she thought she could get away with. She Pulled at the laborer's mind, searching for information. It hit her like a ton of bricks.

35

The Chinese Zodiac had a clairvoyant from the Australian outback, and the woman carried the power of Horse. She had seen their attack coming and warned the rest. In response, the Dragon God had sent their shadow team of elite assassins to prepare a landing party. The laborer was Rooster, and he was their field commander. Not Dragon's replacement, but the next best thing. And the huge soldier next to him was in fact *ex*-military, making him Tiger.

The late Dragon Hero's brother.

Tiger began to stalk forward, moving with perfect silence despite his size. The camo paint on his face and hands rippled as he walked through shadows, allowing him to blend in with the background so completely that he effectively vanished if you took your eyes off of him for a second.

Ivy Pulled harder at Rooster's thoughts, looking for a chink in their armor, for any kind of escape.

Abruptly Tiger wasn't in front of them anymore; seeming to unfold out of the shadows behind Peter, Tiger grabbed the Hero of Sagittarius by the shoulder, spun him around, and slammed a forearm into his face. Peter's nose didn't just break, it *shattered*. Blood sprayed out, and Tiger smiled with genuine pleasure.

Ivy and Karina both gasped at the suddenness of the attack, and Ivy instinctively reached out and Pulled at Peter's thoughts.

Can't defend myself Ivy might get hurt Karina might get hurt can't defend myself Ivy might get hurt Karina might get hurt can't defend myself oh gods this is going to hurt-

Tiger hit him again.

And again.

And again.

11:26 AM PST, June 20, 2015
The Present

"Her heart stopped!"

"Beginning CPR. Someone prep the defibrillator! Dammit, I thought the Heroes were supposed to be stronger than this!"

In an instant of divine connection, everything went calm. Ivy and Karina, Twins in spirit if not in body, reached out their minds to one another and became one.

Ivy Pulled on Snake minutely, forcing his jaws to open wider as they were pressed harder against her neck.

A split second later Karina Pushed Snake hard enough to force his jaws away from her Twin. His jaws had been opened just barely wide enough to Push him away without the added risk of tearing Ivy's throat out in the process.

Rat growled behind Karina and pulled the trigger.

Ivy Pulled on the bullet as it left the gun, and it arced around toward her and drove itself into Snake's shoulder even as he rushed back in to renew his attack. He let out an unearthly howl of pain and stumbled back, blood dripping onto the filthy concrete floor.

Karina lent Snake a Push and he went sailing into the shadows, slamming into something unseen in the back of the warehouse.

The Gemini Twins, at the peak of their abilities in the middle of their month of power, became a whirlwind of destruction. They Pushed and Pulled on each other and the ground simultaneously, rising up into the air and shimmering with a silvery penumbra. Objects from around the warehouse, mostly old tools that hadn't been used in years, were Pulled at random, streaking toward them only to be caught in a controlled Push/Pull that sent them into a spinning vortex around the Heroes.

In this state, Karina and Ivy shared a telepathy so deep that their minds merged, folding into one another.

Protect Peter.

Protect us.

Destroy them all.

Rat and Tiger backed slowly away from the vortex with arms held up to shield their faces, unable and unwilling to get closer. Rat fired his gun in their direction over and over, howling wordlessly the whole time. The Twins simply Pulled the bullets into the vortex and fired them right back out again.

Straight into Tiger's chest.

Tiger grunted, stumbled, then turned tail and ran.

Rat hit a patch of shadows and disappeared.

Throughout the entire display of power, Rooster watched from a distance, not moving a muscle to help his comrades.

He never stopped smiling.

11:27 AM PST, June 20, 2015
The Present

"Ok, we got a heartbeat!"

"But it's irregular. We're not out of the woods yet. Nurse, hand me the syringe."

Ivy's eyes rolled wildly behind lids squeezed shut.

3:22 AM GMT, June 6, 2015
The Recent Past

The Twins Pulled Peter into the eye of their vortex, where he would be safe, at least for the moment. He wasn't moving. They would worry about that after they escaped and got him to a hospital.

"Is nice trick!" Rooster boomed out with a laugh as he dodged a few of the projectiles they sent his way. He did it effortlessly, as if he were tuned in to them. "Last Twins did it better!"

Karina and Ivy shrieked out their rage and Pushed more out at him, while keeping just enough of the detritus within their vortex as a protective barrier should he try any kind of counter attack.

But to no avail. Rooster just kept dodging, nimble and sure-footed, and didn't make any move on them.

Confusion spiked through their mental bond. Ivy chanced a quick look down, and fear tore its way through her and into her Twin. Peter, lying motionless beneath them, was surrounded by a pool of blood. Rooster was simply biding his time, waiting for their friend to die. Waiting to see what would happen to the power of Sagittarius.

The shock of this realization splintered their mental bond, and the Twins dropped heavily onto their feet on either side of Peter. They felt as if they had run a marathon at breakneck speed, which, considering the amount of sheer power they had been flinging around non-stop for the last ten minutes was a fairly accurate analogy.

Rooster took advantage of the moment by drawing a long barreled pistol from a side holster. He leveled it straight it Karina, winked, and pulled the trigger.

Karina Pushed, but she was just so weak. She managed to angle it away from her heart, and the bullet found and shattered her collarbone instead. She let out a soft cry as her body hit the ground, consciousness fleeing as pain flooded through her already exhausted brain.

The Chinese Zodiac general laughed. "Two down! You Americans are weaker than we thought! Dragon god will be pleased." He pointed the gun at Ivy.

With Karina unconscious, Ivy found herself able to do something with their shared power that had never happened before: she drew Karina's Push into herself, joining it seamlessly to her Pull.

She felt both sides of Gemini's power open inside of her, like a flower unfolding its petals. Ivy understood her abilities, and her god, on a level that she had never before even contemplated. She understood her limitations.

In this moment, she didn't have any.

Rooster pulled the trigger, and Ivy Pushed on the bullet inside of the barrel, stopping it cold. The gun exploded in Rooster's right hand, taking a few of his fingers with it. Shrapnel drove itself into his left eye, his jaw, and his rib cage.

Ivy felt every single piece of metal, and she Pulled on it just enough so that it wouldn't pierce any of Rooster's major organs. She wanted Rooster alive, and she wanted him in excruciating agony.

"You tell your Dragon god something from all of us," Ivy said calmly in a voice she didn't recognize as her own. It had a robotic edge to it she had never heard before. "You tell him that if this is the best he can do, maybe he should come himself next time. I'm tired of fighting bitches." Then she viciously Pushed the consciousness out of Rooster's head. He slumped to the ground and blood began to seep from his wounds onto the warehouse floor.

Ivy felt her energy waning, but she shook away her fatigue and dug deep, drawing on the last dregs of her power. The Hero gathered up her will. Pulled Peter and Karina to her and wrapped an arm around each of them. She Pushed a part of her mind out across the ocean, mentally searching for North America, closer, California,

39

closer, San Francisco, almost there, finally the hospital that was specially equipped to administer proper health care to the American Zodiac Heroes.

Ivy gritted her teeth against the strain and Pulled with everything she had.

Everything went black halfway across the ocean.

11:45 AM PST, June 20, 2015
The Present

Feeling returned to Ivy's body first. Even before her mind was consciously aware of her actions, she found herself trying to wiggle her fingers and toes. She was rewarded with slight movement, and a tingling sensation that let her know her body hadn't moved for a while.

She wanted to smile at the return of feeling, but then decided that she wasn't ready for that yet. Maybe later, if and when she had something to really smile about.

As her body continued to wake itself up, Ivy felt cool sheets beneath her. A stiff pillow under her head. And, finally, a minor pinching sensation coming from the inside of her right elbow.

Still in the hospital, Ivy thought. *I wonder how the others are? Did we all make it?*

Sound came next, and Ivy realized that someone nearby was strumming a ukulele.

There, she thought. *THERE is a reason to smile.*

Ivy's eyes cracked open oh so slowly, and she saw exactly what she expected: Peter, mad Hero of a mad god, imbued with a portion of divine power, sitting in a hospital chair with a ukulele in his hands.

Ivy had bought him the ukulele and made him promise to learn how to play it, explaining that it would be a good exercise for his unstable mind. Give him something simple and stable to cling to, like a life raft for his thoughts.

Ivy saw his face and her smile fled. She gasped.

Peter looked up, noticing she was awake, and grinned with the part of his mouth that wasn't still swollen. He easily guessed at the course her thoughts were taking and let out a chuckle that sounded just the slightest bit strained.

40

"What, this old thing?" Peter said casually, raising a hand to gesture at his gauze-wrapped head. "Looks worse than it is. Although my singing has admittedly been a little off key."

Ivy giggled. She simply couldn't help herself. Peter was always too silly not to be caught up in his who-cares style of humor. He would probably be cracking jokes when the world was ending.

Peter leaned forward and his expression turned serious, if still a little wild around the edges. "How are you doing? You and Karina have been out for two weeks."

Ivy ignored his question. "How's Karina? Is she awake? I remember she got shot-"

Peter waved his hand, cutting her off short before she could really get started. "First and foremost, Karina is fine. She woke up about an hour ago and immediately started asking about you. You guys really are twins. And yes, she did get shot, but it wasn't too serious. The bullet ricocheted off her collarbone, which broke in a couple places, but also saved her life. Very little blood loss, although she's still wrapped up in a sling. But hey, you know how us Heroes heal pretty damn fast." Peter paused, eyes going distant for a moment before snapping back into the present. "Let me rephrase that: YOU saved her life. And mine. And your own, of course, although that kind of goes without saying."

A huge sigh of relief bubbled up and out of her, and most of the tension melted away.

Peter plucked idly at the ukulele as he continued: "You and Karina have both been in comas for the past two weeks. The doctors kicked up a fuss about it, but I knew that you just needed to recharge your batteries. You nearly killed yourself Pulling all of us back here to safety. I think I owe you a dinner for that, by the way."

Ivy felt her smile starting to come back of its own volition. "Dinner *and* a movie *and* a beach day."

The mad Hero shook his head, grinning. "You drive a hard bargain, but I accept. Oh and by the way, almost all of the other Heroes have been by to check up on us. I've gotten status reports from most of them. If our little adventure has a silver lining, it's that we finally got through to our entire team how serious this situation is. They're all on standby, every single one of 'em, waiting for orders from you and Karina. If you guys want to push the attack, no pun intended, they'll be there."

Ivy cocked an eyebrow. "What about you?"

41

Peter looked up from the ukulele, locking eyes with her. There wasn't a shred of insanity in his gaze. "I go where you go. Period."

The door banged open, and Karina picked that moment to roll into their room in a wheelchair. Since one of Karina's arms was held immobile against her chest, the Gemini Twin was using her Push to wheel herself around. "IVY!"

"HEY!" Ivy shouted back, romance momentarily pushed aside as she delighted in seeing her Twin safe and sound.

"Did Peter tell you?!"

"About the team? Yeah, he was just filling me in."

Karina shook her head vigorously. "No! Well, yeah, but that's not the point. About Barin!"

Ivy blinked, confused. "What about him?"

Peter leaned over to Karina conspiratorially. "I wanted to let you give her the good news."

Karina offered Peter a high five with her one mobile arm, which he returned with enough gusto to cause her to wince slightly in pain. "Thanks buddy! Anyway, Barin is on his way to a full recovery! The tiny bit of poison that I hadn't managed to Push out of his system knocked him on his ass and damn near into a coma-"

"Everyone gets to have a coma except me," Peter muttered, rolling his eyes.

Karina ignored him. "-but the strength of his immune system combined with his Taurus healing was enough to bring him back from the brink! He's in another wing of the hospital, but he's conscious and getting stronger more quickly than any of us! He'll be out of here in a day, if not less."

"Yay!" Ivy exclaimed. "So we're all ok? Gods above that's such a relief!"

"**Gods above?**" a deep voice boomed out, seeming to come from every direction at once. The lights flickered. "**No. Gods HERE. And you think you've won the battle.**" A huge man, perfectly proportioned like a Greek statue and well over seven feet tall, with shining blonde hair and the beard of a Norse warrior, was suddenly in their midst. Not suddenly as in, just walked into the room. One moment he wasn't there, and the next moment he was.

His name was Gemini.

Ivy and Karina simultaneously opened their mouths to reply, but no sounds came out.

42

Gemini took a moment to glower at each of them in turn. "You have no idea the war being waged here. This war is not for your lives. This war is over the fate of this entire world. The Dragon god has gone rogue, forsaking his animal brethren and bending the wills of the Chinese Zodiac Heroes to accomplish his goals. The Hero of Dragon, and his subsequent death, gave the errant god an opportunity he's been waiting patiently for. You think the Chinese Zodiac Heroes drew you into a fight to try and kill you? The Dragon god drew you into a fight to get *you* to kill his own chosen Hero! For it is only when an American Zodiac Hero kills a Chinese Zodiac Hero that their gods can cross over, rather than have their mantle of power transfer to a new individual. And you *children*," Gemini spat out, disgusted. "have been doing everything in your power to oblige him!"

Peter raised a hand, trying to get a word in edgewise.

Gemini spun on him, and Peter involuntarily shrank back from the god's wrath. "Do not presume to speak to me, son of Sagittarius. You were a mistake from the beginning." He turned back to his own Twin Heroes. "I am here in the flesh because I had no choice. In five minutes you are going to receive a call from the daughter of Aries, reporting that every single one of her Watcher cells has been murdered, to a man. A minute after that, you'll get a call from one of the sons of Pisces, to inform you that his girlfriend has been shot. Do you understand? You are being goaded into action, and you must NOT respond!"

Ivy finally found her voice. "You want us to sit back and do nothing while they kill everyone close to us?!" She hurled at her divine benefactor.

Gemini's fury abruptly vanished. "No, daughters," he replied, voice as cold as the grave. "I want you to kill their gods. All of them."

6/20/15

I can't help but feel like this is all my fault. After getting past the euphoria of all of us getting back alive, along with Barin's recovery, the only thing I can think about is, what was the point? True, I didn't manage to get all of the poison out of Barin's system, and I thought he might die, but I acted so very recklessly in committing me AND my Twin AND Peter into what easily could have been a suicide mission! It's only thanks to Ivy that we're all still alive. And you know what? Barin got better on his own. So our entire mission was a waste of time.

No. No! Even as I write this, I know it's not true. Our mission WASN'T a waste of time! Reckless and rash, yes, but we got even more information about their Zodiac, and we managed to hurt them pretty badly in the process, even though it nearly cost us our lives.

Time to focus on the good, not the bad! And you know something really good? BARIN ASKED ME OUT! I'm giddy with excitement! He's just such a solid guy, with SUCH a huge heart! I just can't wait.

By the by, have I mentioned yet how Gemini wants us to kill the Chinese Zodiac gods? I wonder if Barin has any idea's about that. I think I'll go call him and ask!

Excerpt from the diary of Ivy, Hero of Gemini

6/21/15

My birthday was yesterday, and I completely forgot, due to the whole 'waking up from a coma in the hospital' thing. Then this morning I woke up and the first thing I saw was a vase full of sunflowers sitting next to my bed. A HAPPY BIRTHDAY balloon was tied around the vase. It was so ridiculously sweet. The flowers were from Peter, of course. Surprise surprise, I think I'm falling for him. Big time.

But honestly, that's not what I want to write about at the moment. Nor do I feel like adding my thoughts on my god showing up and demanding that we kill the entire Chinese Zodiac of deities. What I want to write about is how it felt right at the end of that fight with Rooster and all the others. The moment when Karina got shot and Peter was lying on the ground bleeding to death at my feet. At that moment I somehow instinctively knew how to bond Karina's Push power to my own Pull. I felt like I had slipped the limitations of mortality and become a god! The feeling was indescribable, truly. In that moment I could do anything! I WAS gravity! I stopped Rooster all by myself, and he's probably the most powerful Hero that the Chinese Zodiac has right now! Not only that, but I single-handedly brought the three of us back home, saving our lives.

I have never before felt so much like a true superhero.

CHAPTER 4

CANCER

Cancer is represented by a crab, and the metaphysical similarities couldn't be more perfect. Cancers are incredibly strong-willed, and they encase themselves in their own sense of strength like a shell. They are loyal, independent, and self-proclaimed alpha males and females. They can be your best friend or your worst enemy. Sometimes simultaneously.

1:31 PM CDT, June 30, 2015

Edgar looked down. Straight down the 1500 feet from the top of the John Hancock Center skyscraper in downtown Chicago. Looked at the people milling around on the sidewalk. People that looked like a flood of busy ants. And isn't that what they were, most days? Busy little worker ants, scurrying to and fro on one errand or another. Going to work. Leaving work. Dropping off kids. Picking up kids. Desperately just *living*. Each one of them trying to survive another day.

The wind pushed at Edgar, first coming from one direction, then another, trying with mindless abandon to shove him from his perch atop one of the spires. It was an effort in futility; the only thing that the wind managed to shove around was Edgar's curly light brown hair. Every time the Hero of Cancer began to lose his balance, he would turn his body in the direction of the impending fall, and shift himself back into position. Sideways, of course. Edgar's whole life was sideways.

His dark, liquid brown eyes unfocused as Edgar turned his thoughts inward, looking back at the last couple weeks. Opening up his mental file cabinet and examining each memory methodically, all in the name of research. The Hero delved through the attacks from the Chinese Zodiac and their gun-toting proxies with a fine tooth mental comb, searching for details he might have missed, for information that could be useful to his team.

Most of those attacks hadn't been successful. Most.

But not all.

In the immediate days following the incredibly foolish assault on the Chinese Zodiac Heroes on their current home turf in London (*Not foolish*, Edgar amended to himself; *idiotic is a better word*), all of Maddy's watcher cells had been obliterated to a man (*thank the gods she won't really need them again until her month comes around next year*, Edgar

48

thought, examining the memory and then filing it away again). Next, a girlfriend of one of the Pisces Heroes was shot by a lone gunman who had been captured and taken into custody. The girlfriend was still in the hospital, where she had recently undergone two different surgeries to try and remove bullet fragments from her lungs and heart. Doctors didn't know if she would make it, though they were cautiously optimistic. The gunman had managed to kill himself before giving up anything useful.

Then Imani's mother was killed.

Edgar paused at this memory, reviewing what he knew of his teammate. Imani was the young Somali-American Hero of Scorpio, and as the newest fully-fledged member of the American Zodiac Heroes, she was already notorious for leaving her hometown on a whim to go traveling. Imani had just turned 18 last year and received her full mantle of power from her scorpion-esque benefactor, and she instantly developed the wanderlust of a young girl who had just become a demigoddess. More often than not, Imani dragged Brock, the Hero of Libra, with her on her adventures. So when an assassin showed up at her parents house and leveled a gun at Imani's mom, she wasn't there to stop him from pulling the trigger.

Since Imani arrived home to her now-broken family, she hadn't left her father's side.

Edgar filed that memory away again and considered the situation as a whole. The attacks hadn't let up since then, but that was the last time the Chinese Zodiac Heroes had succeeded in getting past their defenses and taken the life of someone close to them. After the funeral of Imani's mother, each American Zodiac Hero in their respective places around the United States had taken it upon themselves to provide round-the-clock security for their loved ones. And on top of that, Edgar and Alex, Heroes of Cancer and the only Heroes in the American Zodiac with abilities akin to teleportation, had offered to be on call day and night for anyone who needed them. The Gemini Twins collaborated with them and set up a telepathic on-call service, connecting all of the other Heroes with the Cancer boys (*Cancer MEN*, Edgar thought with a wry grin).

The infuriating part? Providing defense was all they were doing. The Chinese Zodiac Heroes were the ones pressing the offense in this war. And it *was* a war, no doubt about that.

What were the American Zodiac Heroes doing about it? NOTHING. Not since the Gemini Twins and Sagittarius had taken the fight to the Chinese Zodiac and nearly lost their lives.

--*Edgar*-- the voice slipped behind his primary thought stream. Came in sideways, so to speak, which was how he knew it was his fellow Hero Alex and not one of the Twins. When Karina Pushed a telepathic thought at you, it came directly to the front of your mind, instantly getting your attention. The Cancer men were much more subtle.

Cancer telepathy worked much like their pseudo-teleportation ability: they couldn't make direct contact, because that went against the M.O. of their god. Rather, they could mentally communicate through 'sideways-speak', as they called it. Slipping their thoughts sideways into the minds of others. It was difficult using this with regular people, because if a person was concentrating about something else hard enough, Cancer sideways-speak wouldn't be strong enough to get the person's attention.

But for conversations between the two of them, who knew exactly what to be on alert for, it was perfect.

--*Yo*-- Edgar sent back to Alex. The strength of the mental broadcast was weak enough that he knew Alex was somewhere in the south, presumably in his hometown of New Orleans.

--*Busy?*--

Alex wouldn't have asked telepathically if everything was copacetic. Edgar's body tensed as he replied --*Nope. Need me?*--

--*Bourbon Street. Regulars.*--

'Regulars' was a code word; it meant that Alex didn't think it was another attack from the Chinese Zodiac Heroes. Just a normal, everyday riot. Maybe even something gang related. Edgar instantly called up his mental file on New Orleans and remembered that there was in fact a turf war going on between two rival mob families, the Matranga's and the Provenzano's. The Matranga brothers had pushed the Provenzano family out of New Orleans in the early 1900's, but the descendants of the Provenzano's were back, and they had long memories.

Edgar filed all of this information away again and turned his body to a 90 degree angle relative to the direction of Alex's mental broadcast. The Hero of Cancer closed his eyes, concentrated, and *shifted.*

There was a sensation of rushing air screaming past his ears at mach speeds, and then the wind abruptly stopped.

The screaming didn't.

Edgar opened his eyes and found himself on the roof of a jazz club that sat right in the center of the long stretch of Bourbon Street, arguably the most famous street in all of New Orleans. Parties here were bigger, approaching hedonism. Wealth was put on ostentatious display by those who had it. And *everything* was mind-wrenchingly colorful.

Edgar was instantly assaulted by an ocular cacophony in all the colors of the rainbow. Bright flags hung proudly from every business and hotel that marched off in both directions, giving Bourbon Street a cramped, yet cozy, atmosphere. Even during the day the multitude of neon signs never turned off. The sheer wattage required to run all of those neon beacons day and night created an electric feel to the air. Edgar swore he could feel the metal fillings in his teeth vibrating slightly in response to the static discharge in the air.

But the most prevalent color at this moment in time was red. The street below was filled with men of various ethnicities but only two loyalties, and they were each doing their best to dispatch those that stood on the wrong side, subjectively speaking. By the gods, there was blood *everywhere*.

Alex stepped up next to him on the roof. Edgar had been so taken aback by the assault on his senses that he hadn't realized his brother-in-arms was already there. Worry was painted across Alex's handsome face as he surveyed the carnage happening on the street below them.

At 6'3", Alex towered over Edgar, who stood a head and a half shorter at 5'8". However, despite the dissimilarity in height, they had remarkably similar builds. Both were avid body builders as was befitting their station as heroic demigods; on the taller Cancer Hero Alex, it made him look somewhat like a tank. On the shorter Hero Edgar, it gave him the appearance of a silverback gorilla, compact but with arms thick enough to bend steel bars.

Edgar had dark brown eyes, the kind that poets describe as 'soulful'. Alex's eyes were like chunks of blue-green ice, hard and unyielding one moment, blazing with passion the next. Both Cancer Heroes had brown hair; Alex chose to keep his short and neat like a soldier, whereas Edgar preferred it long and curly, with a matching

51

beard. Today, as per the norm, both were wearing jeans and tight shirts. Not only for showing off their rippling muscles, but because loose clothing impeded their matching fighting style.

The gang war raged on in the street below them, in broad daylight no less, as the two rival mafia families attempted once and for all to wipe the other off of the map. The screams that Edgar had originally thought to be coming from victims caught up in the fray were actually, upon further inspection, coming from the mafiosos themselves. Edgar looked closer and saw that they were going at it with bladed weapons rather than guns. He saw thugs wielding knives and machetes, and, in the hands of one particularly big brute, a two-handed sword that looked like it was taken right off the set of Braveheart.

"Why no guns?" Edgar asked curiously, turning to Alex and arching an eyebrow.

"I mentally probed them before I called you. Seems they had a war council and decided to do this old school. More brutal this way," Alex replied with a disgusted shake of his head.

"Cops?"

Alex pointed down the street to the northern entrance of Bourbon Street, where it intersected with Esplanade Avenue. Edgar saw a blockade of police cars with lights running, but no sirens. "Set up a cordon, but they aren't interfering. Too smart for that."

Edgar nodded. "Smart enough to wait for us, at least. Plan?"

"Contain, disarm, disable. Try not to kill them. Cops can sort the whole thing out later."

Enough said; they went to it with the ease of old war comrades. And why not? Edgar and Alex were among the elder of the American Zodiac Heroes, Alex being 36 and Edgar, 33. They had been using their powers for over a decade without pause. If the American Zodiac Heroes had true front line fighters trying to make a difference, it was the Cancer men.

The two Heroes turned and *shifted* off of the rooftop, appearing in the middle of the warring mafioso henchmen. Their appearance caused a stir of confusion, and they took advantage of the slight pause to *shift* rapid-fire between individual Sicilians, Italians, and New Orleans natives, disarming them and breaking limbs to discourage further bloodshed.

A few seconds later and they had disarmed over half of the thugs. Some turned and ran, terrified of this new threat that they could barely track with the naked eye. Most recognized that the Heroes represented a danger to all of them regardless of which crime family they belonged to, and attempted to face them head on.

Unfortunately for the bad guys, the Cancer Heroes didn't operate on a head-on basis.

Over a dozen of the thugs attempted to form a cohesive battle line, bristling with sharpened weaponry, to take down the Heroes so they could get back to their honest gang war.

Edgar, now armed with knives of his own (unwillingly given to him from men who were now on the ground clutching broken arms and wrists) *shifted* sideways around and behind the criminal line in a crouch, slicing through hamstrings and ankles like a hot knife through butter. The criminals fell, howling in pain and anger.

The last mafiosos standing, still armed and uninjured, finally got smart and drew back into a circle facing outwards.

--*They're learning*-- Alex sent to Edgar. This close in proximity, Edgar not only heard the words as clearly as if Alex had spoken out loud, he also caught the undertone of amusement.

--*Not quickly enough. Time to pop the balloon. You take the left side, I'll take the right.*--

The Heroes *shifted* themselves into position opposite each other with the circle of bad guys between them, gave the thugs a quick look at the direction they were coming from, and, more importantly, the height they were coming from, and then turned and *shifted* sideways into the group.

Halfway through the *shift*, even as the criminals were oh-so-slowly stabbing outwards at where they expected the Heroes to be, the Cancer men dropped down into sideways slides that took them between the legs of the circled criminals and underneath the porcupine of metal being held out at chest height. Once under, they minutely adjusted their angle of *shift* in concert and spun in a tight circle of their own, reaching out with their knives to slice through the backs of knees.

They *shifted* back out as the entire circle of men fell to the ground.

Through unspoken agreement, the Cancer Heroes shifted once more to the top of the jazz club roof, staring down at the bloodshed (*MILD bloodshed, considering,* Edgar thought) that they had wrought.

Less than five minutes had passed since Edgar had arrived.

53

"Thanks for coming," Alex said, barely out of breath, eyes still on the men beneath them. "I'm going to go tell the police they can-"

"Hold on," Edgar interrupted, peering closer. "Did we miss one?" He pointed down into the mass of downed men as one of them climbed back up to his feet on legs that very obviously weren't injured. Nor did his arms appear to be broken in any way.

Alex squinted down at him. The man appeared at first glance to be one of the Italian gangsters; no way to tell which crime family he gave his allegiance to. And yet, as Alex stared, the man's skin began to ripple, becoming darker in color, taking on a more golden hue.

The man's clothes, a gray three piece suit with a blood-red rose in one of the buttonholes (*a bit cliché for a mobster in this generation*, Alex mused to himself) were also beginning to change. The suit jacket and shirt ran together like wax, melting away until all that remained was the black vest covering the man's bare chest. The slacks went from gray to jet black, ballooning out slightly at the ankles. Shoes and socks melted away, leaving the man in bare feet.

"Who the hell..." Alex muttered under his breath, before casting his mind out and trying to slip sideways into the strange man's mind.

The man looked up at them and grinned. His smile was full of broken, yellowed teeth that looked like fangs. With a wink and a wave, he suddenly bolted, running straight for the police cordon at the far end of the street faster than any human could run.

Alex cursed loudly and with the skill of a sailor.

Edgar was still tracking the running stranger. "Chinese Zodiac Hero?"

"Monkey. Shapeshifter. Heading for my apartment."

The Cancer men *shifted* in tandem to the rooftop at the end of the street, above the police cordon and just ahead of Monkey. A full two dozen of New Orleans finest stood behind the five police cars blocking the street, and each of them had a pistol or shotgun leveled at the oncoming threat. Except that the policemen below didn't yet realize they were facing down a demigod from a rival Zodiac.

Edgar drew in a deep breath. "**EVERYONE DOWN!**" he bellowed. The police took one look at him, and, recognizing him as one of the Cancer Heroes, hurriedly obeyed.

54

Meanwhile, Alex *shifted* down to the street and stood directly in Monkey's path, blue-green eyes blazing, fists held up before him in a tight boxing stance. Monkey, standing at Edgar's height but skinny as a rail, grinned all the wider and rushed him. Alex threw a quick one-two combo of jabs, meaning to put Monkey off balance more than hurt him. Monkey flowed underneath the pumping fists and opened a mouthful of teeth that closely resembled razors, and, bending his neck at an unnatural angle, tried to take a bite out of Alex's stomach. Alex saw it coming and *shifted* to the left a foot, then came right back in with a swift roundhouse kick that should have taken Monkey's head off. Again Monkey evaded him, body bending and flowing under the kick, moving more like a liquid than a solid. And again Monkey immediately moved in for a counter-attack.

Back and forth the rival Zodiac Heroes fought, each looking for an advantage, and each finding none to be had. It had the look of a dance more than a fight. It would have been a thing of beauty if not for the fact that each man wanted the other dead at his feet.

Worried that joining the fight could cause more harm than good to his fellow Hero, Edgar instead cast his mind out and made contact with the Gemini Twins.

--Monkey is here. New Orleans. Alex is fighting him. It's a stalemate. Thoughts?--

Karina responded immediately, Pushing her thoughts directly into his mind. It was a shock, being used to sideways telepathy as he was instead of direct contact.

DON'T KILL HIM! Edgar could hear the urgency in Karina's mental broadcast.

--Don't know if we could.-- Edgar responded nervously, eyes glued to the scene below him. Neither had yet to score a hit on the other. *--Monkey is a shapeshifter. Alex can't land a hit. For the moment, neither can Monkey.--* He frowned. *--If we can't kill him, what do you want us to do?--*

Could the two of you contain him, even for a second? Karina's mental voice had gone from urgent and fearful to eager.

Edgar remembered all the times he and Alex had worked, specifically when they focused on synced up fighting moves. One move, in particular, that was meant to trap an opponent rather than hurt him...but would it work on a shapeshifter like Monkey?

--I think so.--

55

Then we have an idea. Can you give me an exact location of a spot within ten feet of where you can contain Monkey?

Edgar concentrated on a patch of asphalt close to the two fighters, neither of whom were showing any signs of fatigue, and mentally broadcast it across the States to where Karina was sitting in a living room with her Twin and one of the other Heroes local to San Francisco.

Perfect! she sent back. *Ok, for this to work, we need to time it perfectly. Here's the plan...*

Edgar listened, nodding and growing more excited. The instant Karina broke her link, Edgar turned his attention Alex and mentally sent him two words, --*Get ready.*-- and a picture. Alex didn't break stride in the fight, but Edgar felt him telepathically confirm.

Monkey, though not tiring, was getting frustrated. Alex could read this on the shapeshifter's face as plain as day, and he used it. Without warning, the Cancer Hero went into a flurry of motion, launching his strongest attack yet. He threw punch after punch at Monkey, each one appearing to be coming in full force, but each little more than a feint, meant to keep Monkey as off balance as possible.

For the first time becoming a trifle unsteady, Monkey took a single step back in retreat.

Alex instantly *shifted* away, and then back at a slightly different angle. In the same moment, Edgar finally *shifted* down from the rooftop, coming at Monkey from the other side.

The result was the two Cancer Heroes pressing the diminutive Monkey between their powerful bodies. The breath rushed out of Monkey as his ribs ground against one another before he had a chance to restructure the inside of his body. The pain unnerved him. Monkey was used to delivering pain, but never feeling it himself.

Another body hit the ground five feet in front of Monkey.

Enter Andy, the Hero of Leo, chosen vessel of the lion goddess.

Edgar and Alex each grabbed one of Monkey's wrists, and went into a precisely maintained half-*shift* away from Monkey, stretching the Chinese Zodiac Hero's arms out wide and keeping enough pressure that he couldn't change his shape.

Andy stepped forward, right hand held out to one side. Monkey stared as claws popped out of Andy's fingertips.

"Nice trick," Monkey snarled, unafraid. "We have a guy on our side who can do that, too. Have you met Rat? He's planning on killing your wife and eating her heart while you watch."

Andy smiled, unfazed by the threat. "I've heard of Rat, and his unfortunate eating habits. But can his claws do this?" As he spoke, Andy's claws blazed red-hot. Before Monkey could react, Andy closed the distance between them, raised his burning hand high, and slashed down with all the strength of Leo.

Monkey's left arm hit the ground with a sizzle of burning flesh.

Before Monkey even had a chance to scream, Alex wrapped him up in a bear hug and *shifted*. The two of them vanished.

Alex reappeared a second later, alone.

Andy's smile grew wider. "Where'd you put him?"

The Cancer Hero shrugged his muscular shoulders. "Facedown in a ride paddy in the middle of a rural part of China. Seemed appropriate for a Chinese Zodiac Hero. Not to mention the fact that most of their team is actually in England."

"Nice!" Andy extended his right hand, claws once more safely retracted, and shook with both of them. "Now if you wouldn't mind, could you let the Gemini Twins know that we're done here? I doubt that Monkey or Rat could make good on that threat against my wife anytime soon, but just to be on the safe side..."

"Of course," Edgar said warmly. He mentally broadcast to Karina that they had neutralized Monkey without killing him and that Andy was ready to come home. Then the three of them said quick goodbyes and, just like that, Andy was flying off in the direction from which he had arrived, waving at them until he was out of sight over the western horizon.

"So," Edgar said casually. "do you want to talk to the police about this one, or should I?"

Alex realized they were still standing in front of the police cordon, where New Orleans finest were just starting to poke their heads up to assess the situation.

"I'll do it," the big Hero offered. "My hometown, after all. You should go check on your girlfriend, make sure she's ok."

Edgar laughed. "Did you forget that my girlfriend is a cop, and knows Krav Maga, Israeli street fighting? She probably could have handled Monkey better than we did!"

Alex tried to smile and failed, hearing the forced quality to his friend's laughter. No matter how good she was, she was still human. Of course he would want to check back up on her as soon as he got home, but at the same time, if you couldn't laugh at a time like this, it could end up crushing you. As they say, you gotta laugh to stop the tears.

"Anyway," Edgar went on, "there's something that we have to talk about sometime soon. All of us, I mean. Karina said we can't kill them, because it will release their gods into our world. But she also said that Gemini *wants* us to release their gods, right? So that we can kill every single one of them, and end the bloodthirsty reign of the entire Chinese Zodiac?"

Alex nodded.

"That means that we're going to have to kill the Chinese Heroes sometime. But has anyone figured out how the hell we're supposed to kill one of their gods, let alone *twelve* of them?"

"That was one of the details that Gemini left out, wasn't it?"

"Yeah. Pretty damn big detail, too," Edgar said, all traces of humor gone from his voice.

"Honestly, I've been racking my mind about it, and I have absolutely no idea. But we **will** figure it out. In the meantime, we do what we've always done, and what we'll continue to do after this war is over."

Edgar, catching his thought, nodded firmly. "We protect those who can't protect themselves, standing firm on the front lines."

"Shoulder to shoulder, until our shift is ended," Alex finished.

They shook hands and went their separate ways, both knowing in their hearts that their shift could only end one way.

Death.

Excerpt from the diary of Edgar, Hero of Cancer

7/1/15

I think I'm going to break up with my girlfriend. I jokingly told Alex that hey, she's a cop, she knows Krav Maga, she can handle herself, no big deal, blah blah blah, but the truth is that ever since this war of the Zodiacs started, I can't stop worrying about her. She's only human, and that's exactly who the Chinese Zodiac is targeting. Gods know I love her. I just want her to be safe.

As long as we're together, I know in my heart that she isn't safe. And since I volunteered to be on call for any and all emergencies, that means that she goes unprotected for long stretches of time.

Right now it really sucks to be a demigod.

Excerpt from the diary of Alex, Hero of Cancer

7/1/15
I'm worried about Monkey. I don't like killing, but I don't shy away from it when it's necessary, either. And I know that Monkey needs to die. Period.
The threat that he presents is monumental. Yes, Andy crippled him, and yes, I dropped him off in a remote region of China, but the man is a demigod just like we are. He's not going to be trapped in China for long, and when he finds his way back here, he's going to be looking for revenge.
I have to figure out a way to kill Monkey AND his god at the same time, before he can do any more damage. I won't let him hurt anyone else.

CHAPTER 5
LEO

Leo is the sign of the lion, and has the unusual combination of being one of the fiercest zodiac signs, as well as one of the calmest. While those may seem like opposing ideas, the explanation is simple: a Leo will calmly go with the flow and roll with the punches right up until a distantly established breaking point. Once that line has been crossed, however, there's only one thing you can do: get the hell out of the way.

9:27 PM PST, July 27, 2015

Nearly a month had gone by with no attacks from the Chinese Zodiac faction. For the first couple of weeks after the mob brawl in New Orleans, the entire American Zodiac team had remained on high alert, positive that it was a ruse of some kind, meant to lure them into complacency and let their guard down.

All remained calm.

The Gemini Twins had cautiously attempted to mentally probe around England, trying to catch a hint of the Chinese Zodiac Heroes, or even the Dragon god himself.

Nothing.

And so, for the first time since this had all begun just a few short months ago in the Aries temple, the American Zodiac Heroes had started to hope that maybe, just maybe, this whole thing was blowing over.

That didn't mean that they weren't still on edge. The Cancer Heroes continued to make themselves available should any crisis pop up. The Gemini Twins maintained a mental connection with each team member.

Meanwhile, the other Heroes began to relax, day by day.

For Andy, the Leo Hero who had so recently been called into glorious battle, relaxing meant getting together with best friend and fellow Hero Peter for a nice night of video games.

Of course, you wouldn't think it was so relaxing if you could hear the dialogue flying back and forth between the two.

Andy: "Ahhh, stop killing me! We're on the same team!"

Peter: "But you were in the way! Your sacrifice was not in vain!"

Andy: "Oh really? We'll see if you feel the same way when you're hurtling towards a fiery death!"

62

Peter: "You stay the hell away from me!"
Andy: "C'mere, you need a helping hand over that cliff edge!"
Peter: "Aaaaaaaaaaaaahhhh!!!"

And so on. Anyone passing within a three-block radius of Peter's sizable apartment located in the eastern hills of San Francisco would have thought there was an actual war going on within. That someone would have been shocked to learn that two of the most powerful beings on the planet were simply playing Super Mario Bros.

They were sitting on opposite ends of the black leather couch situated right in the middle of Peter's living room in his two bedroom apartment that he lived in by himself. Three of the four walls in the living was crowded with bookshelves. Peter had been reading and collecting books since his childhood and he now proudly displayed his own personal library. The bookshelves on the east wall groaned under the weight of an impressive collection of fantasy ranging from Robert Jordan to Brandon Sanderson, Margaret Weis to Tracy Hickman. The west wall was crowded with science fiction, starting with Dune on one end and finishing with The Hitchhiker's Guide to the Galaxy on the other. Peter wasn't much into alphabetical organization. The north wall showed off Peter's comic book collection, as well as a smattering of historical fiction like Shogun. The south wall, something of a black sheep in Peter's library, held the TV, various video game consoles, and a random assortment of movies.

The two best friends had identical frenzied looks etched upon similarly handsome features. Each held a controller tightly, though Andy was taking very special care not to get too worked up and clench the controller too hard. What most people didn't know was that one of the side effects of carrying the torch of Leo was that your body became an actual torch; inside Andy's chest, in place of a heart, was a miniature sun that pumped plasma through his veins. During past video game sessions with Peter, Andy had gotten so worked up during game play, his body temperature had risen high enough that the controller had literally melted to slag in his hands.

On the outside, however, Andy looked very much like any other human; you wouldn't be able to tell that he was a demigod just by looking at him. Andy had close-cropped light brown hair combed in a side-part and a very precisely trimmed beard of matching color. Light brown eyes stared intently at the TV screen. Expensive clothing clung to every inch of his slightly chubby body: black leather shoes, gray Calvin Klein slacks, white dress shirt, gray sweater. All this just to play some video games. Everywhere Andy went, he dressed to the nines. And if his enemies underestimated him at face value due to his potbelly and cherub cheeks, they were in for one hell of a surprise: underneath that extra layer of weight, Andy packed just as many muscles as the rest of the demigods in the American Zodiac.

Peter was a study in contrast: while he had an almost identical muscular build, he didn't carry around any extra weight on top of it, and his clothing options were the polar opposite of his well dressed teammate. Hairy legs were sticking out of tattered blue gym shorts, while a tight black tank top desperately tried to contain his sizable pectoral muscles. Peter's thick arms bulged as he wrestled with his video game controller. Tattoos covered almost every inch of exposed skin that had never seen the sun long enough to get tan. His long curly brown hair and beard were sticking out wildly in every direction. And his eyes...well, Peter's dark brown eyes rarely blinked these days.

The current level they were playing ended (with both of them alive, for a change) and they took a short break to grab a couple beers out of the fridge.

"So, how are things going with Ivy?" Andy asked, following Peter into his kitchen. "Has she started moving in yet?"

Peter grunted in amusement as he opened the fridge and perused the contents within. "Well, we spend most nights together, but she hasn't officially moved in, no. Still currently lives with her Twin, Karina. Technically." Peter snagged two bottles of stout and popped the twist-tops off, handing one to Andy.

Andy gratefully accepted, clinked his bottle against Peter's, and took a long pull. The Hero of Leo belched appreciatively and wiped foam from his immaculately trimmed mustache. "What are the Gemini Twins up to? Still monitoring everything, just in case?"

The mad Hero of Sagittarius nodded. "Just in cases."

"How do they do that, anyway? Isn't it exhausting?"

Peter barked out a laugh. "For us demigods? Nah, it's a walk in the park for them. As far as Ivy explained the process to me, she keeps a constant low-level mental Pull on all of our teammates, right at the very periphery of our thoughts. You know, so she doesn't pick up anything she doesn't want to hear." He winked. "In the event of an emergency, thought patterns go wild in your brain, anyone's brain, and Ivy picks up on that. She zeroes in, picks up all the pertinent details, and feeds them to Karina. As the Pusher, Karina then makes mental contact with the person broadcasting the emergency, Pushing her thoughts into their mind. In this way, Karina and Ivy set up something like a three-way telepathic call to ascertain the extent of the emergency and the kind of help that's needed. Just like last month, when they mentally connected with the Cancer Heroes in New Orleans and then were able to send you in to help."

Andy took another swig, thinking about that. He held up a hand as something occurred to him. "Hold on a sec. The Twins need to be in the same room for this to be completely effective, right?"

"Correct-a-mundo."

"But you said that Ivy spends most of her nights here these days. How do you keep the Hero network going during those nights?"

Peter nodded his head in the direction of his fully furnished spare bedroom. "When Ivy comes here, so does Karina. Recently Barin has been coming along, too, ever since he and Karina started getting a little more serious. Really makes this place feel more like a home if I'm being honest, having all these people around." Peter paused and chugged down his beer. As he turned back to the fridge to grab a fresh one, he threw the empty bottle over his right shoulder. The bottle went sailing end over end through the air and landed in his recycling bin in the far corner of the kitchen. Peter kept right on talking over his shoulder at Andy, not even acknowledging the skillful throw he had just made. "Ya know, before this I had never really had the opportunity to spend much time with Barin, but he's a pretty badass guy. Really down to earth. His Taurus aura actually has kind of a calming effect on my madness." Peter turned around with a fresh beer in his hand, letting the fridge slam shut behind him.

"First of all," Andy said. "that was a great throw." He glanced in the direction of the recycling bin to punctuate his point.

Peter shrugged. "Nah, that's nothing. I just don't miss, that's all."

Andy laughed. "Well, it's still cool to watch." The laughter faded away, and the Leo Hero's features drew down in a serious look. "There's something I wanted to talk to you about, friend to friend. This superhero life, flying in to the rescue, it's not for me. As much as I'm glad I was able to help out in New Orleans with the thing with Monkey, it's not something I want to make a habit out of."

The two friends wandered back into the living room and sat down on the couch. For the moment, they left their controllers alone.

"For someone who doesn't want to be a superhero, you're pretty damn good at it," Peter pointed out.

Andy shook his head. "It's different for you, man. You're dating another Hero. You're both on the same level, leading similar lives. Whereas I married a human, and happily I might add. Do you have any idea what that's like? How much I constantly worry that some kind of backlash might land on her instead of me? It's the reason why I try to live a normal, *human* life. Human career, human schedule, nice home in the suburbs, a couple of dogs. *That's* the life for me. And that's also the reason why, when you invite me over to hang out with you and Ivy and the other local Heroes, I always have an excuse not to."

There was a long beat of silence while Peter mulled that over.

"I absolutely respect your feelings about this," Peter said at last, speaking slowly. As slowly as he could, at least. "But don't you think you were chosen for this for a reason? One of our gods hand-picked you!"

"Goddess," Andy interjected with a wry grin.

"Goddess, right. Anyway, I, for one, think the lion goddess made a damn good call! You have the strength to carry this mantle of power, and I'm speaking more about your strength of mind, as well as your moral compass! You're a good person, buddy. A *great* person. The kind of person that can step up and make a difference. And on that note, I have to hit the bathroom. But we're not done talking about this!" Peter popped up off of the couch like a champagne cork and headed off in the direction of the master bathroom in the back. Andy heard him start whistling to himself as the door shut behind him.

Andy smiled, taking another sip of his beer. The Hero glanced at his Rolex and noticed how late it was getting. *I should call Lindsay and check in, see if she-*

That was as far as he got before something struck his mind with the force of a meteor. It wasn't one of the Gemini Twins trying to establish telepathic contact. It wasn't even one of the Cancer men from farther off. No, this was much more primal.

It came from the direction of his house, located roughly five miles east of Peter's apartment.

When Peter strolled out of the bathroom a few minutes later, still whistling, Andy was gone.

The Leo demigod raced through the streets in his black BMW, driving like a madman. For the first time in his life, Andy wished he was more powerful. Wished that he had complete super-speed, instead of just being able to speed up in short bursts.

The miniature sun that beat in Andy's chest was pounding rapidly against his ribcage. White-hot plasma poured through his veins like lava erupting furiously from a volcano. Andy's body temperature had risen so much that he was literally smoking. The steering wheel beneath his hands had started to melt, growing soft in between his clenched fingers.

In the five miles of curving, hilly streets between Peter's apartment and his own townhouse, Andy ran no fewer than three drivers off the road. They honked their horns and threw curses and threats at him. Andy was blind to them, and deaf to their horns and screams.

What felt like several lifetimes later, Andy finally pulled up into his driveway. Leapt out of the car before it had even come to a complete stop. The BMW ended up in his wife's rose garden. Andy didn't notice.

A final burst of speed took him up the porch steps and through the front door, where he stopped short.

Blood.

Andy saw, but at first his mind didn't register exactly what he was seeing. The blood was *everywhere*. Blood stained the once-white living room carpet. Blood splattered across the beautiful yellow drapes hanging in front of the picture windows. Blood dripped down from the ceiling.

Andy took a hesitant step forward, and his foot kicked something that slid a few feet before coming to a stop against an overturned blue vase.

It was an arm.

A delicate, porcelain-white left arm.

Andy's eyes travelled the length of it, starting at the grotesquely torn flesh around the knob of shoulder bone down to the fingers that had curled into a claw in rigor mortis. On the ring finger was a platinum band that supported a large, flawless diamond.

Andy remembered buying that wedding ring.

Remembered sliding that ring onto that finger in front of friends and family.

Grief tore its way through Andy's entire soul, shaking his world apart at the seams. He dropped to his knees in a pool of blood that immediately began soaking into his gray slacks, pulling the arm to him and cradling it to his chest like a child clutching a favorite doll. Fiery tears streamed from his eyes, evaporating against the heat of his body before they made it even halfway down his cheeks.

A floorboard creaked.

Andy looked up, and there was his wife standing in the kitchen doorway. There was Lindsay. Standing in front of him, *alive*! Alive and smiling beatifically and...missing her left arm.

Understandable Andy thought, trying to force sense into everything that was happening. *Of course she's missing her left arm, because I'm holding it right here, and if I can just put it back on her, everything will be fine.*

But why was she smiling? People who have just had an arm torn off of their body don't smile!

She's smiling because I'm here, and she knows I can fix this Andy's gibbering mind insisted, hysteria rising within him like a tempest. *I can fix this, of course I can!*

Lindsay opened her mouth, but the voice that came out didn't belong to his wife.

"An arm for an arm," a thin, reedy, but undeniably masculine voice grated out of the thing that looked like his wife.

Andy dropped the arm.

"At least, that was my original intent," the voice continued, making a mockery of Lindsay's facial features. "But when I started, I couldn't just stop at an arm! Who could? So then I took a few fingers. One of her ears." The *creature* giggled, and the sound was like nails on a chalkboard. "Then she stopped screaming, so I ripped out her tongue."

Andy climbed to his feet. His expensive Calvin Klein slacks were stained a dark burgundy. He didn't notice.

"Then she died. Humans bleed out so quickly! I got irritated with her for dying so fast, so I cut her head off. I left it in your bed, if you want it back."

The creature pretending to be Andy's wife saw the look in his eyes, and used Lindsay's face to smile broadly. A ripple started at the corner of that smile and spread across Lindsay's body. An instant

68

passed, and it wasn't Lindsay anymore. It was a small, stick-thin Arabian man.

Monkey.

The smile never left Monkey's face. "I killed your bulldogs, too. It took you so long to get here, and I was so bored! But don't worry, I put them in bed with your wife's head. So she won't be lonely. I did that for *her*. You're welcome!"

All the color drained out of the world to Andy's eyes. All except the red.

Claws popped out of Andy's fingertips, glowing and smoking.

Monkey tittered, rocking back and forth on his bare feet. "Oh, I remember those claws! But where are your friends to hold me down?"

Andy opened his mouth and roared. All of the anguish and pain in the universe poured out of him. And, just for a moment, the confident look on Monkey's face faltered.

Andy shot forward, claws outstretched, aimed right at Monkey's throat. The lion Hero moved with a burst of inhuman speed, calling upon every ounce of power that was raging through him.

And yet, somehow, Monkey evaded him.

Andy couldn't check his speed in time and crashed through the living room wall, falling to the black and white checkerboard tile floor in the kitchen. He landed in blood. His wife's torso was lying only inches away from him.

Monkey landed on his back, curled his one bony arm around Andy's neck, wrapped his legs around Andy's stomach, and *squeezed*. For such a tiny man, there was strength enough in Monkey to bring a down a bull with that chokehold.

Andy tucked his chin down into Monkey's arm, buying himself just barely enough space to breath. He opened his mouth, which was suddenly filled with the sharp teeth of a lion, and bit down on Monkey's forearm.

Monkey shrieked and tried to disengage. He succeeded, but left behind a big chunk of ropey muscle in Andy's mouth.

For the first time in Monkey's life, since acquiring the power of Monkey from the previous Hero (by hitting him from a distance with poisoned darts until he stopped moving), Monkey was well and truly afraid. This was followed by something else happening to him for the first time: he turned and ran for his very life.

Andy was on his feet and chasing him down before Monkey had gone more than half a dozen steps.

Monkey veritably *flew* out of the front door and into the chilly San Francisco night.

Andy followed, smashing out of the front picture windows, shards of glass exploding outward in every direction.

Monkey leapt gracefully over the stalled BMW in the rose garden.

Andy went *through* the BMW, leaving two smoking pieces of car behind him glowing a sullen red where he had plowed through.

Monkey used his shape shifting ability to darken his skin and clothing, trying to camouflage himself and disappear into the night.

Andy, the Hero of the lion goddess, had eyes that worked better at night than in the daytime. He had no trouble tracking Monkey despite the attempted camouflage.

Monkey tried a new tactic, heading west, out of the hilly residential area and toward downtown, hoping to lose Andy in traffic. As more and more cars appeared on the streets before them, Monkey took a page from the Chinese Hero Rabbit and bounded over each vehicle, while constantly shifting his body and clothes to blend in with everything around them. Most of the drivers didn't even realize he was there.

Andy called upon his short-burst enhanced speed to dodge silently through the traffic.

With each passing second, Andy drew closer.

Ten feet away.

Seven feet.

Three.

With a final burst of speed, Andy shot to one side of the street, then leaped forward at an angle. He caught Monkey in a bear hug in midair, and wrapped together they smashed down into a parked minivan. The minivan shattered apart around their bodies. Drivers and pedestrians alike finally noticed that there were demigods fighting in their midst. All around, people began to scream. And run. As far away as they could possibly get.

Monkey, momentarily dazed, didn't struggle as Andy got to his feet with the Chinese Hero still held tight to his chest. Andy *squeezed*...and Monkey felt his spine break. The little Arabian man suddenly couldn't feel his legs anymore, and that was when panic flooded through his mind and shook off the cobwebs.

Too late.

Andy opened up his mouth, still bristling with fangs, and darted his head forward. His powerful jaws clamped around Monkey's neck, tightened, yanked. And just like that, half of Monkey's neck was gone. Blood fountained out of the gaping wound. Monkey tried to scream, but he had no more vocal cords to scream with.

He died silently, still trying to figure out where he had gone wrong.

Andy was about to let go, when he felt the presence of his goddess right next to him.

"**You mustn't let go,**" she whispered into his ear. And then she told him exactly what to do. The last thing she said before her presence vanished was "**If you do this, you will have peace.**"

Then Andy's divine benefactor was gone, and something inside of Monkey's body was stirring.

Just like when Maddy had killed the Dragon Hero months ago, the Monkey god himself was climbing free from his mortal confines. A blacker-than-black shadow of an enormous monkey was clawing his way out of the ruined body.

Andy wouldn't let go.

"**Little mortal,**" a rasping voice called out from within the inky black shadow. "**do you truly think you can stop me from entering your world?**" The body of the Arabian fell apart in Andy's arms, and he found himself holding a living, writhing shadow. It grew with each passing second. Andy wouldn't be able to hold on for much longer.

"You took my wife from me," Andy gasped out, straining with all his might. "you took everything that I hold dear on this earth!"

The shadow smiled. "**Not everything. Not yet.**" It got an arm free, an arm that ended not with a hand, but with a spike.

Andy didn't blink, didn't flinch.

The Monkey god drove his spiked appendage straight into Andy's heart with all his considerable strength.

The last thing Andy ever saw on this earth were the eyes in the Monkey god's face widening, realizing too late that he faced a Hero who didn't have a heart in his chest; Andy had a sun. A sun that was powered by the pure, unfiltered fire of a goddess.

Liquid white fire raced up the shadowy arm, wrapped around the Monkey god's body, consuming it from the outside in. Unearthly howls poured from his throat as he burned as bright as a star. It was over in seconds.

Andy's final thought before darkness claimed him was *I'm coming, Lindsay. I'm coming, my dearest love.* He smiled and let the world fall away.

CHAPTER 6

VIRGO

Virgo is the 6th sign on the American Zodiac wheel, and serves as the natural leader of the group. More than anything else, this sign was born to lead through serving those around them. The two traits most commonly attributed to Virgo are attention to detail and an innate understanding of things. Virgo is the begrudging leader, who only accepts the reigns of control when forced to, and that is what makes them competent and, above all, compassionate.

6:00 PM PST, August 27, 2015

It was exactly one month after Andy's untimely death. One month after the brutal murder of his wife at the hands of the Monkey Hero. One month after the downfall of the first of the twelve Chinese Zodiac gods.

It was only right that they have Andy's funeral on such a momentous anniversary.

The American Zodiac had gathered at Golden Gate Park, in one of the immense grassy fields on the west end. The entire park had been shut down for this event, with the San Francisco police department brought in to monitor the barricades set up at each entrance. If the Chinese Zodiac made a move, the police would serve as little more than an early warning system, but it was better than nothing.

Peter, the Hero of Sagittarius and Andy's best friend, stomped up onto the stage that had been erected for the funeral. Andy's body was in a closed coffin behind him, a beautiful casket made of cherry oak rather than the usual pine. Even in death, Andy dressed to the nines. The sky overhead was thick with clouds, dark purples and grays shot through with veins of silver. It seemed appropriate.

Peter grabbed the microphone that had been set up in the middle of the stage in between two blown-up portraits: the picture on the left was of Andy and Lindsay together. It was one of their wedding pictures, and the newlyweds were smiling broadly, head over heels in love and overflowing with happiness. The one on the right was a solo picture of Andy, dressed in a gray suit and wearing a silly grin on his face. Peter took a long beat to study the two portraits, his hands tight on the microphone stand, squeezing so hard his knuckles turned white.

When Peter turned back around to face the rest of his teammates, many of them involuntarily shrank back from the wild look on his face. His eyes were darting rapidly back and forth as if he was searching for someone to unleash all of his emotions on. Peter's lips pulled back from his teeth in a feral snarl. Ivy, sitting in the front row, came halfway out of her seat, clearly wanting to help. Peter locked eyes with her and shook his head minutely, cords of muscle standing out in his neck. He mouthed the word 'No'.

Seconds passed and the tension built. The clouds directly above Peter started to churn, growing black. Lightning danced through the sky, feeding off of the energy Peter was unconsciously discharging out into the atmosphere. Finally, just when Ivy was ready to leap onstage and try to help whether Peter wanted her to or not, the mad Hero took a long, shuddering breath. His eyes squeezed shut and a tear slid down one cheek, disappearing into his tangle of beard.

"It shouldn't have been him," Peter rasped out into the microphone. The speakers on either end of the stage carried his words clearly to all of those mourning with him in the audience. "Andy didn't want this. He just wanted a normal, human life. That's the last thing he told me before...before..." Peter's shoulders heaved, and tears began to pour from his eyes, still clenched shut. "It shouldn't have been him," Peter whispered, then whirled around and walked quickly off of the stage. Ivy jumped up from her chair and caught up with him a dozen yards away. Peter collapsed into her arms, shaking, while Ivy made soothing sounds.

An uncomfortable silence began to build among the rest of the Heroes. They looked around at each other, waiting for someone else to take the stage. In the front row, a six-foot-tall blonde woman named Ariele climbed slowly to her feet. Ariele was the reclusive Hero of Virgo, and the only reason she was there was because Ivy had begged her to come. Pleaded with her to finally take her rightful role among them. It had taken over an hour, but Ariele had finally allowed herself to be convinced.

Now here she was, about to speak at a funeral for a teammate that she had never even met. As the statuesque Hero mounted the stage she desperately tried to work moisture back into her mouth, which had gone as dry as a desert from her skyrocketing nervousness.

"I didn't know...Andy," Ariele began with a slight stutter. The tall, nearly Amazonian blonde paused a moment to fiddle with the microphone stand, buying herself a moment to get her thoughts in order. She cleared her throat a few times, nerves standing on end as she unwillingly took on the role of public speaker. "I wish I had. Really. Um. Ivy told me that he was an awesome guy. Honestly, it wasn't until right before I stepped onstage that I realized that many of us, well, some of us, at least, have never met before this moment, despite our common, um, link."

Out in the audience, the American Zodiac Heroes found themselves nodding along, feeling a sense of shame rising within them. They were a team, together one of the most powerful forces ever assembled on the entire planet, and they barely knew each other's names, let alone each other's faces.

Ariele paused, cleared her throat yet again, took a sip of water from the bottle she had clenched in one hand. Her mind flashed back to a week ago, when she had gotten a call from Ivy, her best friend. And, she admitted to herself, one of the only Heroes she cared about.

> Ivy: Hey.
> Ariele: Hey.
> Ivy: How are you?
> Ariele: I'm ok. You?
> Ivy: Struggling. Andy was Peter's best friend, you know?
> Ariele: I know. *Pause* Look, I'm really sorry I didn't call sooner, it's just-
>
> Ivy: It's ok. Really, it is. I understand. I hate to even make this call, because you know what I'm gonna ask you to do, and you know I wouldn't if it wasn't such a serious-
> Ariele: I know.
>
> They both laughed as they felt the old friendship telepathy taking over, making the conversation easier. Telepathy that had nothing to do with superpowers.
>
> Ivy: We need you, Ariele. All of us. We need a leader.
> Ariele: *Sigh* I'll be there. I guess we both knew this day would come. Is it ok if my boyfriend comes?
>
> Ivy: Chris? Of COURSE it's ok! Every single one of us is bringing significant others and family members along. Can't be too careful these days. Bring your sister Kaitlin, too! I haven't seen her in WAY too long.

Ariele came back to the present, scanning the crowd in front of her. She picked out a couple of the Heroes that she had met in passing, recognized a few others from pictures. Each Hero had a cluster of humans around them: mothers, fathers, siblings, boyfriends, girlfriends, best friends. Nobody wanted to be far from their human family.

In the back corner Ariele saw the youngest member of their team, Imani, the Hero of Scorpio and barely 18 years old. Imani's father sat on one side of her with his arm around her thin shoulders. On her other side sat a short blond man with a thick beard and thicker glasses. He could only be Brock, Hero of Libra and self-proclaimed mentor of Imani. Ariele remembered Ivy telling her that Imani's mother had been murdered recently in a Chinese Zodiac attack. She felt her heart breaking; tears threatened in the corners of her eyes, and she fought down a sob.

"One of our own is gone, and I didn't even know him," Ariele continued, eyes downcast. She gulped. "To be honest, I didn't want to know him. I haven't wanted to know many of you. Not because I thought I wouldn't like you, but because I thought I'd like you too much. And because of what I thought you'd all ask of me." Ariele looked up and caught the gaze of her boyfriend Chris, and her sister, Kaitlin, who were sitting in the front row. They both stared, unwavering, and she felt their love and support flowing into her. Ariele firmed her shoulders, and raised her eyes to the rest of them.

"Over ten years ago, when I turned 18, I was visited by my goddess. I'm sure that sounds familiar: I've heard that most if not all of us have gotten visits, and many of them happened on our 18th birthdays when we received the full mantle of power from our respective deities." All hint of a stutter disappeared from her voice.

Ariele's teammates were nodding their heads, remembering their own experiences.

"My goddess told me that I was destined to be the leader of our team, and that terrified me. Who am I to be asked, to be told, to be the leader of a group of demigods?" Ariele paused again, took a deep breath. "I was so scared of that responsibility that I actively avoided meeting most of you. I thought that if I never met you, then you would never have the chance to ask me to lead you. How arrogant is that? To assume that after meeting me you would all be falling over yourselves wanting me to be president of our little club!"

The tears were threatening again, but she didn't try to hold them back this time. "Because of my arrogance, I never got the chance to meet Andy, and now he's gone from us forever. And from what I understand after talking with Ivy and Peter, our lion Hero was an amazing person. Kind. Caring. Generous. Loved by all who met him." The tears began to spill over. As she looked out into the audience, she saw that she wasn't the only one crying.

"I'm not standing up here now saying that I want to be your leader. I'm simply saying that I'm ready to join the fight. Maybe if *all* of us had jumped in before this point, then Andy would still be alive. Now, unfortunately, we'll never know. But what I do know is that I have special abilities, just like the rest of you, and I'm ready to help. Not just for Andy's sake, but for all of us." Ariele stared out at the somber group in front of her, unflinching, meeting the eyes of every one of her teammates. "I'm really excited to finally meet all of you."

As Ariele stepped down off of the stage, she was met by her boyfriend who immediately wrapped his arms around her. The tears were pouring down her face now. When Chris pulled away, she was stunned to see all the Heroes standing around the two of them, waiting with open arms. For the first time in what felt like too long, a smile tentatively stretched across her face.

By the time the funeral was over, Ariele was completely drained. But instead of heading to her hotel room with Chris and going to sleep (which was all she wanted), she instead sent Chris and Kaitlin off with the other human families to a different part of the park where a light dinner would be served and got down to business with her team.

It was time to plan an end to this war.

As nobody wanted to head indoors, the Heroes had a few picnic tables set up, and their own dinner was served by a catering staff that was on hand for the funeral. It was a simple fare of sandwiches, chips, and an assortment of fruit. All Ariele cared about was the coffee that came with it.

The first order of business was, at Ariele's request, everyone simply meeting each other. They were a team; it was time to start acting like one, and that meant knowing who your teammates were. Ariele had also asked if anyone minded if she took down some notes about everyone to better coordinate what they all could do and how they could work most efficiently together. Everyone agreed. At the end of the day, Ariele's notebook with her hastily scribbled notes looked something like this:

Aries: Maddy. Age 22. Lives: San Francisco, CA. Lynx familiar. Lynx also spear; magical. War Hero. Strength, speed, endurance. Field general?

Taurus: Barin. Age 31. Lives: SF, CA. Turn skin to stone. Mind to stone, too (mental defense). Can turn others to stone w/ touch. STRENGTH!

Gemini: Ivy. Age 30. Lives: SF, CA. PULL.
          Karina. Age 32. Lives: SF, CA. PUSH.

Cancer: Edgar. Age 34. Lives: Chicago, IL. Older brother of Aquarius Hero (Eli).
          Alex. Age 37. Lives: New Orleans, LA.
          Sideways shifting (nearly teleporting). Sideways telepathy.

Leo: Andy. Deceased. Killed Monkey God with sun heart (needs further study).

Virgo: Ariele. Age 30. Lives: Jackson Hole, WY. Auto analysis, 360 degree perspective, Command voice.

Libra: Brock. Age 31. Lives: Salt Lake City, UT. Balance power (use against Chinese Zodiac gods somehow?).

Scorpio: Imani. Age 18. Lives: SLC, UT. Darkness manipulation, projection.

Sagittarius: Peter. Age 30. Lives: SF, CA. Never misses. Some psychic abilities, extent unknown. Transformation? Strength?

Interesting Hero: appears mad and doesn't know full extent of own powers. Can't figure out???

Capricorn: Sally. Age 29. Lives: SLC, UT. Climbing and phasing, one at a time. Can split body in two, one mind, use both powers.

Aquarius: Eli. Age 30. Lives: New York City, NY. 'Better vibe'. Psychic AND physical application. Genius intellect. Younger brother of Cancer Hero (Edgar). Only Heroes who are actually related. Interesting.

Pisces: Max, Quinton. Ages: 23. Lives: SLC, UT. 'Good' ability: charisma, pos. energy, agility. 'Bad' ability: metaphysical mask of darkness (deathmask). Speed. Strength. Shadow manipulation?

At everyone's request, Ariele agreed to print out a copy of her assessment of each of the Heroes and hand it out to everyone so they could learn each others abilities. After that, Heroes began exchanging phone numbers. Addresses. Ideas.

Ideas!

A thought grasped hold of Ariele's mind, causing her to trail off whatever she had just been saying to Ivy and Karina. A thought that was so extraordinary in its simplicity that she couldn't for the life of her figure out why she hadn't thought of it before.

"What?" Ivy asked, noting with some alarm the way her friend's gaze suddenly just drifted off into the distance.

Ariele shook her head. "Sorry. Nothing. *Everything.*" She jumped to her feet. "**HEY!**" she had shouted before she even realized what she was doing.

All of the other Heroes stopped their conversations on the spot and turned toward her. Ariele realized with a start that this was a funeral and everyone was on edge and jumpy...and here she was yelling at everyone.

Well, too late to be nervous or embarrassed now. The only thing to do was to forge ahead. "Sorry. Let me start by saying that there's no emergency. It's just that I had an idea I wanted to share."

80

They all visibly relaxed at the words 'no emergency', and the looks of fearful anticipation on each face was replaced by one of curiosity.

"We've all been sharing who we are and what we can do. Well, as most of you know by now, I have an auto analysis ability. But truthfully, I haven't really explained what that means. It means that I can look at something, or hear something, and instantly understand everything about it. For example, you've all shared the basics of what you can do. It's all we've had time for, really. But just in sharing that little bit of your ability, I know every single little detail about who you are and what you can do. Normally I don't tell people that I can do this, because people have a tendency to get weird around me, and assume that I know all of their secrets. Let me assure you, this is not the case."

"Thank the gods!" Peter shouted drunkenly from the back, where he'd been talking with the Cancer men. Polite laughter rippled across their group from one end to the other, a tiny audible wave.

Ariele smiled. "In your case, Peter, I *do* know your secrets." She turned and winked ostentatiously at Ivy, and Peter blushed so deeply he nearly burst into flame. This time the laughter was louder.

"Anyway," the Virgo Hero continued, getting back on point. "I thought that as much fun as this meet and greet is, maybe it's time to get down to business. What I propose is to push all of the tables together and have a candid group discussion about what is going on with the Chinese Zodiac Heroes and their animal gods, and what we can do, as a team, to put an end to it. I'm going to try and use my analysis power to observe our team as a whole and maybe figure out ways we can combine our abilities for maximum efficiency."

Ariele got unanimous agreement almost immediately, which surprised her. It really made her feel like she was taking control, providing direction and guidance. It felt...*amazing*.

As the Heroes began rearranging the picnic tables and pushing them together, Ivy pulled her to the side, out of earshot of the others. "I *knew* you could step up!" Ivy said, obvious pride threaded through her words.

Ariele blushed almost as deeply as Peter had. "I'm not trying to be a leader. I'm just trying to help," she protested weakly.

Ivy grinned. "*That's* why you're the perfect choice. Look at everyone." Ivy swept a hand out to indicate all of the Heroes, already working together. "They've known you for just a few hours, and they're ready to follow you. And so am I."

Ariele drew her best friend into a hug. "Thank you," she whispered.

Ivy pulled back, grinning from ear to ear. "Are you kidding me? Thank *you*!"

"Hey boss!" A deep voice interrupted them. They turned to see all of the other Heroes already seated and looking at her expectantly. The speaker was Brock, the bearded Hero of Libra whom she'd just met for the first time today. He winked at her. "We're ready when you are!"

Ariele and Ivy rushed over to the group, and so began the most casual war meeting that has ever taken place in recorded history. The Heroes launched into a lively discussion of their various abilities, which abilities might best compliment others, the fights some of them had already been in, the Chinese Zodiac Heroes they'd met, strengths, weaknesses, ideal battlegrounds, thoughts about how to kill the Chinese Zodiac animal gods, on and on and on...

At one point Ariele tuned out their words and instead listened in on what her auto analysis was telling her about these people. The full extent of each individual ability. The strengths and weaknesses of her people.

Her people.

Ariele focused on individuals, and let information flood into her. When she finished with all of them, she began to study them in pairs, and now she was mentally inundated with how those pairings of abilities would work together...

An idea was forming, but it was just beyond the periphery of conscious thought.

Once Ariele had considered all the pair combinations, she took another mental step forward and began to study them in different combinations of three to a team, then four, then five...

The idea took shape slowly, resolving itself within her mind like a polaroid being shaken to produce the picture hidden within.

Finally, she looked at her team as a whole, cohesive unit. Observed, ironically, that they almost looked like the famous painting of the Last Supper. Noticed how Brock, the bearded Libra Hero, was sitting dead center, straight across from her. Looking at him from a certain angle, he appeared to be the hinge that held them together. Or the spear point that drove them forward...

Ariele's eyes grew wide.

It was then that she noticed the conversation had died. Every eye was on her.

Ivy, sitting to her left, leaned over and put a hand on her shoulder. "What? What did you see?"

"I know how to beat them," Ariele whispered. Karina, sitting on the other side of Ivy, gave Ariele's words a little Push so that everyone could hear. "I know how to beat their Heroes, and their gods." Ariele looked to her left, to her right. Met the eyes of her people seated there around her. Felt a connection with each and every one of them, a connection that strengthened as she looked at them. Lastly, her eyes came back to rest on Brock.

"You will be our savior," Ariele proclaimed.

Brock leaned back in his chair, propped his feet up on the edge of the table, and grinned.

Excerpt from the diary of Ariele, Hero of Virgo

8/27/15

I am exhausted but happy. I know that sounds terrible to say, considering I just came from a funeral, but it's true. The service we held for Andy was beautiful, and it served to bring every single one of the American Zodiac Heroes together for the first time (at least, the first time in this generation). And you know what? When I think about Andy and Lindsay, I can feel them at peace. I believe that the goddess Leo welcomed them to an eternal place of bliss. Call it heaven or nirvana or whatever you want, all I know is that I can feel them both smiling down upon us.

The true reason for the smile on my face as I write this is simple: I'm a leader now. I feel like I've been fighting this my whole life, and yet now that I've accepted and embraced it, I feel whole. I spent the day meeting everyone from the American Zodiac, and they are amazing people!

We are going to win this war. I can feel it.

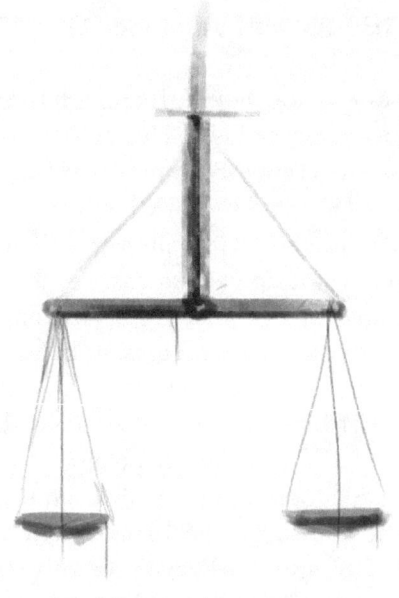

CHAPTER 7

LIBRA

Libra is depicted as the scales of justice, and that is exactly what the Libra represents: being just. Fairness to them isn't an option, it's a way of life. To be a Libra is to know balance. To be the Hero of Libra is to force that balance out into the universe.

7:39 PM PST, October 13, 2015

"So you're our savior, huh?" Imani, Hero of Scorpio, teased from across the indoor soccer field. Her naturally loud voice reverberated around the empty stadium. Imani was the teenage child of Somali expatriates. She had recently lost her mother in an attack from the Chinese Zodiac, and while she was still very much grieving over it, she tried to cover it up with sarcasm and being a smartass. Imani was a diminutive waif of a teenager, standing just shy of 5'6", and had long, straight black hair and eyes so brown they were almost black.

Brock, Hero of Libra, ex-army specialist who had been dishonorably discharged for disorderly behavior, supposed savior of the American Zodiac Heroes and possibly even the world, didn't even blush. " I think 'messiah' is probably a better title!" he shouted back at her. Brock, 5'8" and stocky with an impressively long blond beard, very much looked like a wise, older mentor. He liked to fling his beard over one shoulder and harrumph at Imani, acting like an ancient Chinese martial artist guru teaching a young whippersnapper student who never paid attention. He threatened that one day he would get a tall walking stick just so he could smack Imani over the head with it when she wasn't paying attention.

Imani made a gagging sound, then without warning spun in a tight circle and whipped out a hand, hurling a ball of pure, inky darkness at her friend and mentor.

Brock calmly held his ground, not flinching as the shadow ball flew straight and true, directly at his face. At the very last second Brock raised his right hand palm up toward the ceiling. The light issuing forth from the halogen lights above their heads instantly went from a particulate state to a liquid state and poured down into Brock's waiting hand at his mental command. Liquid light took solid form in the shape of a brilliantly glowing baseball bat, and the Hero of Libra took a mighty swing. The light bat hit the shadow ball and both exploded outward with a sound not unlike a sonic boom.

86

Brock automatically protected himself from the magical shrapnel by nullifying the blast as it touched his body. Imani, however, lacking his combat instincts even after months of training, didn't do anything to protect herself before the shock wave had lifted her from the ground and thrown her from the field of lime-green astroturf and into the orange plastic stadium seating behind her. She hit the third row with a *CRUNCH!*

Brock shook his head in exasperation and trekked across the fake grass to make sure she was ok.

Again.

Imani was climbing to her feet as Brock walked up, as ungainly as a newborn colt. Blood trickled from numerous shallow cuts and gashes on her body, and one of her skinny arms was bent backward at an unnatural angle. Even as Brock looked on, the blood pulled back into Imani's slender body, the cuts sealed themselves up, and her arm straightened with a sickening crack that made him cringe.

"How many times do I have to tell you?" Brock began for what felt like the hundredth time.

Imani held up her hands to forestall him. "I know, I know! I can't rely on my healing ability to protect me. I have to learn how to protect myself as if-"

"-as if you didn't have a healing power," he finished for her with a stern look. "You know we don't have a full read on the Chinese Zodiac Heroes, or their animal gods. What if they have someone like me on their team, someone who can mess with other Heroes powers?"

"I *know*," Imani said again, eyes on the ground, shoulders hunched in. She looked every inch the penitent pupil.

Brock reined it in, reminding himself that Imani was only a teenager. He had just had his 32nd birthday a week ago, and despite his own relatively young age, Brock was feeling older than his years these days. War had that effect on a person when they were on the front lines, forced a person to age rapidly, at least on the inside.

He changed the subject. "That shadow ball you threw was impressive! That's the biggest one I've seen you throw. I honestly didn't think you'd be able to make one that big, considering that I've got all the lights on in here. Where did you get the shadows to make it?"

Imani looked up, grinning, sensing that she had been forgiven. "I learned how to densify and expand my shadows!"

"Densify? That's not even a word." Brock stroked his long beard and tried to look imperious as he stared down his nose at Imani.

"It is, too! I looked it up last night when I was learning how to *densify* my shadows!"

Now it was Brock's turn to throw his hands up, this time in defeat. "Alright, alright!" he said with a laugh. "So how'd you figure it?

"I'm not one hundred percent sure," Imani admitted with a shrug. "I just know that it feels like I'm pushing the shadow into itself, then drawing it back out, bigger and darker than before. Almost like I'm kneading dough. Does that make sense?"

Brock stiffened, but tried not show it. It sounded like she had learned how to make pulsating black holes by collapsing her shadows into themselves. What would have happened if her shadow ball had touched him? A shiver worked its way down his spine.

Imani didn't notice, and was past the subject and onto something more exciting. "What about you?! How did you make that light bat?! You've never done that before, you always just nullify what I do! I mean, you don't even really have a-" She cut herself off, blushing furiously. Her eyes once more dropped to the ground.

The demigod chuckled. "Don't really have a power? I know, I really don't. What I have is a set of scales. So far I've shown you that I can nullify your power by making you as powerless as I am. However, I can balance the scales in another way: I can make *me* as powerful as *you*."

"Really? Why haven't you done that before now?"

Brock shrugged his shoulders, dropping down lightly into one of the undamaged orange plastic chairs on the row Imani had crash landed on. After a second's consideration, Imani sat down, too.

"Because until now, you've needed a safe environment to practice in, not only to build your power but to build your confidence. Surprise surprise, we don't have time for that anymore. Now you need to learn how to use your power against someone who fights back."

The Libra Hero glanced over at his young friend to see if his words were getting through. Imani sat there, not moving, staring straight ahead. It almost looked as if she wasn't even breath-

Brock shot to his feet, head on a swivel, trying to look everywhere at once to see where the threat was coming from. Old army instincts kicked into high gear.

The stadium was still empty.

Silent.

He turned back to Imani only to see that she wasn't alone.

To her right sat a diminutive, bald Asian man with an ageless face. Ageless in the way that at first glance, he appeared to be in his thirties. But one look at his eyes and Brock would swear he was 3000 years old if he was a day.

To Imani's left, in the chair Brock had recently vacated, sat his divine benefactor. Libra herself, the goddess of balance.

Like the other gods and goddesses of the American Zodiac, Libra was well over seven feet tall and, befitting her station, was dressed in the shapeless, dark gray robes of a judge. Dark auburn hair fell in ringlets over a heart-shaped face. Light gray eyes stared piercingly at him, and he felt himself being weighed and measured before her.

The tension of the moment shattered into little pieces when the little Asian man sneezed.

"Apologies, but I have never before been in this country, and I fear something in the air disagrees with me," he said in Chinese, and somehow also simultaneously in perfect English.

Brock raised an eyebrow, and opened his mouth to enquire about it.

"Yes, I am speaking Chinese, and yes, you are understanding me perfectly," the stranger said before Brock could get the question out. "And no, before you ask, I cannot read your mind. However, I can see into the future far enough to see you decide to ask me about your understanding of my language. I am answering you before you have the chance to ask in order to save time. Which we do not have much of."

"Time?" Brock asked weakly. He felt control of the situation slipping away from him.

"Correct. I have taken us to a moment slightly outside of time, you see, and I do not think that my compatriots would appreciate me doing so. Which is one of the reasons why I have secured the help of your benefactor." The stranger nodded to Libra, who was still staring holes through Brock. "Not, however, the main reason."

89

"Which is?"

"I felt I had a better chance at getting you to listen to me if I had support. To answer your next question, the reason I'm here before you is because you will know I am not lying, whereas one of your compatriots might not trust me so easily. You humans are not a very trusting group, I've found, particularly Americans."

"But aren't you-"

"Human? Only in the loosest sense of the term. I am the Hero of Dog, of the Chinese Zodiac. I am the first and only Hero to have carried the power of Dog throughout all of history, and as such, my god's power and influence have grown within me until we reached a...convergence...of minds. I am the closest any of the Chinese Zodiac gods have come to crossing over into your world. At least until your war Hero released the Dragon god. That was a very egregious mistake."

Brock sat down heavily on the edge of the seat behind him, struggling furiously to process and comprehend everything that was being thrown at him.

First and foremost, Dog was right. Brock *did* know that he was being honest with him. One of the fringe benefits of his abilities was to weigh the words of those around him and sift lies from truth.

"Brock."

He looked up into the eternal eyes of his goddess.

"He is here to help us understand. Our Zodiac is filled with beings that you name gods, and while we may be beings of extraordinary power and wisdom, we are not omniscient." Libra spoke softly, her voice deep and resonant, and Brock felt her compassion washing over him in a psychic wave. **"We knew the threat that the Dragon god represented, but we didn't know the *why* behind that threat. Which is precisely why Dog is here."**

Brock nodded, seeing the perspective of his entire Zodiac as Libra opened herself up to him. During the flash of insight he gained from the link with his goddess, Brock came to understand something that chilled him to the core: Libra was afraid. They all were.

If the Dragon god was enough of a threat to scare the very gods that had given Brock and his friends their powers to begin with, what did that say about the situation?

"Please," Dog said. "we MUST hurry. Will you open your mind to me, and hear my story?"

Brock took one more look at Imani, sitting frozen in time between two of the most powerful entities in the universe. "Yes."

As the ancient Chinese Zodiac Hero began to speak, Brock closed his eyes and dropped his mental defenses, allowing a psychic landscape unfold within his mind.

"Every myth you've ever heard is true. The American Zodiac and the Chinese Zodiac are but two threads in a vast pattern that stretches across all of time and space. Norse mythology, with their home of Asgard, is real."

Brock saw images of a vast, shining temple set atop a mountain peak. Surrounding the temple on all sides was a sprawling metropolis that stretched out beyond the horizons. Men and women, as large in proportion as his own gods and goddesses, roamed the crisscrossing streets in colorful clothing. A lightning bolt tore across the sky, and within that bolt of light Brock saw a huge blond man with a massive hammer held in one outstretched hand.

"The Greek and Roman pantheons of gods and goddesses are real."

Massive deities in flowing, multi-colored robes flashed through his mind, faces stern and strong, yet kind. Their skin appeared imbued with golden light that pulsed outward, giving the whole scene a sense of beatitude.

"Japanese kami, Irish Tuatha-de-danann, Native American spirits and spirit walkers, every god, demon, and entity that has ever before existed in myth and lore, *all are real*."

Pictures and tableaus flickered through his mind faster than he could latch onto them. Brock caught glimpses of a heaven filled with puffy clouds, a fiery pit that stank of sulfur, planes of green grass, wild animals, winged faeries, pixies, dryads, faster and faster until Brock feared that his mind would snap from input overload. Brock's conscious mind began to buckle, but understanding still broke through on a deeper level than he could consciously comprehend.

"What is important is that all have withdrawn to their own worlds, to their own devices. All except for my Zodiac. And yours."

An entire celestial kingdom burst into his mind. Brock understood that he was looking at the world that his goddess came from. An undivided society of beings as powerful as the twelve gods and goddesses seated on the American Zodiac. The kingdom was built out of pure starstuff. The sky above was a living mosaic of constellations, breathtakingly beautiful to gaze upon. The streets that the beings walked upon were chiseled from dying stars and still glowed with ambient light. The entire kingdom pulsed with light.

This picture was followed by a glimpse at an ancient land of rolling hills, towering mountain ranges, and verdant valleys that would one day be called China. A land that was ruled over by a single benevolent being, and his twelve animal spirit disciples upon whom he granted divine wisdom.

"Our world overlaps yours, closer than any other mythological or divine kingdom. We were once as much a part of your world as we were of our own. Such was the strength of that overlap that when humans came and took over, establishing themselves as rulers over their own land and pushing our influence out...part of each one of us stayed behind. Was cut away."

Brock felt the pain of that separation, deep within his own soul. He felt as if he were being spiritually torn in two. He longed to cry out in anguish, but he clenched his jaws and opened his mind further. He needed to bear witness to *everything*.

"Your own gods and goddesses *chose* to give part of themselves to you, their Heroes. Those of us in the Chinese Zodiac were forced. The part of ourselves left in the human world joined with twelve humans, who would become our first Heroes. Many of us found peace in that joining. Myself, Horse, a few others, we eventually found happiness with our gods in the ability to be a part of both worlds."

Brock felt the pain of the separation fade away as a new awareness took its place. He realized that awareness came from joining with human counterparts.

"The Dragon god never found peace, not for a single moment. Part of that comes from the fact that he has the weakest overlap with your world. You see, dragons don't exist in this realm. In our kingdom, Dragon is one of the most powerful among us. In your world, however, his Hero was one of the weakest."

Brock felt the rage of the Dragon god, white hot and unforgiving, twisted with a cruel insanity. He shuddered, and sweat beaded on his forehead.

"The first Dragon Hero, overcome with madness, began killing indiscriminately. You see, even as the weakest Hero, the fact remained that he was still a human imbued with the power of a god."

"Why didn't the rest of you stop him?!" Brock burst out, unable to contain himself any longer.

The Hero of Dog looked at him sadly. "He was our brother. As terrible as he was, we couldn't bring ourselves to destroy him." The diminutive man sighed. "As it turned out, we didn't have to. Eventually, a young man in the village the Dragon Hero was living in took the murderous Hero by surprise. Killed him. Dragon himself, over in our world, exulted in the death. He assumed that once the mortal vessel carrying part of his power, part of his *soul*, was killed, then that part of him would naturally cross back over to our spirit kingdom.

"He was wrong."

Brock saw, in his mind, the young Asian villager killing the first Dragon Hero. Saw a dragon-shaped shadow wrench itself free of the dead body and force itself into a new living vessel.

"That was the first time one of us passed into a new human body through bloodshed. As you already know, it was not the last. Since that time, our mantles of power have switched hands many, many times. All except for mine own."

Brock mentally witnessed thousands of years slipping by like a whirlwind of time. Saw the bloody path that each subsequent Chinese Zodiac Hero forged, through China and beyond, spreading across the entire Eastern hemisphere.

"That bloodshed echoed across from your world into ours. Slowly, my Zodiac...my brothers and sisters...became as corrupted as their villainous Heroes, some more than others. Each began to lust for power in their own way, and encouraged the killing of Heroes through a twisted reasoning of wanting to find the strongest human vessel worthy of their power."

Brock felt the corruption spreading through the ranks of animal gods and goddesses, felt it like a cancer was spreading through his own body.

"Over the years, the Dragon god's goal changed. He realized he wasn't going to be able to get that missing piece of himself back, and so he began to search for a way to fully cross from *our* world into *yours*. As you know, he has accomplished that goal."

Brock had only heard the story of Maddy killing the British Dragon Hero; now he saw it firsthand as it unfolded within his mind.

"Since that event transpired, more of us began to desire to do the same. To be killed by an American Zodiac Hero and so break

93

the symbiotic link between Heroes and gods and be of one body again...suffice to say, even I was tempted."

Dog trailed off for the briefest of moments, considering...

"But then Monkey's Hero was killed. He and Dragon were never very close, in our world or yours, but Monkey always secretly supported Dragon's goal, longing to see if it could be done. When it happened, when Monkey began crossing into your world, only to be struck down by the power of your lion goddess and her brave Hero, we all felt it. A psychic shockwave rippled back across into our world and tore through every single one of us, as well as through our current Heroes. As I said before, regardless of corruption, we are still family. Connected at the deepest levels.

"Why do you think there have been no attacks since that happened? The Chinese Zodiac Heroes are *terrified*. Not only of your group, but of their own divine benefactors! The Dragon god is keeping a tight rein on his closest associates, whom I believe your group have already met, but the rest of us have scattered and gone underground."

The link between the two Heroes abruptly vanished, leaving Brock reeling in place, struggling to regain his bearings. As his vision finally cleared and he came fully back to the present, Brock found both the Hero of Dog as well as his own goddess on their feet. Despite Dog's diminutive form, he seemed to tower over Brock, much as Libra did.

Brock found his voice at last. "What do you want me to do?"

Dog stared evenly at him, black eyes unblinking and fierce. "I want you to go to your group and tell them all that I have told you, much as I hope that your goddess will go to her Zodiac and tell all of them. I want for my fellow Heroes to be spared, if possible. It's not too late for the corruption in our ranks to be cleansed. And I want the Dragon god to be destroyed, once and for all. He has no more place in this world, or any other."

Brock tried not to act daunted by the task that lay before him. "What's the Dragon god's endgame?"

Libra answered him, the compassion in her voice replaced with an edge of concern. **"Your world is the gateway to *all* worlds. Earth itself is the plane of existence at the very heart of all reality. The Dragon god seeks to find a new world for himself through some lost doorway."**

"What kind of world?"

"One that believes in dragons," The Hero of Dog said sadly. "And he will happily burn your world to ashes in his search for it."

10/13/15

Oh. My. Gods. I feel like some kind of combination of drunk, stoned, and possibly tripping out of my mind on psychedelics. I still can't really believe what happened. I've met Libra before, once, when I turned 18, but to see her show up out of the blue with the Hero of Dog and then go on to show me EVERY DAMN PANTHEON OF GODS AT ONCE AND TELL ME EVERY SINGLE ONE OF THEM IS REAL?! Oh, and then to fill me in on the Dragon god's master plan, that was great. I especially loved the part where THE WHOLE WORLD IS NOW AT STAKE BECAUSE DRAGON IS A LITTLE BITCH AND IS ALSO CRAZY!

Deep breaths. Deeeeep breaths. It's gonna be fine. Know how I know that? Because I'm the savior for some reason. Yup. That's right. Last month our brand new leader pointed a finger at me and said guess what, you're gonna be the one who saves the day. NO PRESSURE OR ANYTHING!

I need a drink.

CHAPTER 8

SCORPIO

Scorpio is a creature of moonlight and shadows, and is ruled by a passion unlike anything the world has ever seen. On the good side of this coin, we see a Hero who wants to heal the world. On the bad side, we see a Hero who wants to shroud the world in darkness.

9:59 PM PST, October 31, 2015

Imani's heart beat an irregular staccato rhythm in her chest as she sped down the tight corridor, shoes slapping loudly on the linoleum. Above her head, multi-colored strobe lights pulsed, splashing her shadow on the walls around her almost in time with her-

Movement!

Barely registering the attack in her conscious mind, Imani gave herself over to her newly trained instincts and threw herself flat. She heard a rush of air as something big passed swiftly over her, smashing into the far wall.

Bounding back up to her feet, the just-turned-19-year-old demigod continued her headlong rush without looking back, breathing heavily. A blood-streaked door appeared on her left and she dropped her shoulder down, reaching deep into the reservoir of power within her core. Imani's shoulder flashed black as shadows hardened around her, and she smashed through the door and into an inferno. A scream bubbled up to her lips as living flames reached for her with open arms-

30 minutes earlier...

"And you *promise* this isn't some extra test you whipped up just to mess with me? Like, crazy Peter isn't hiding in there waiting to freak me out?" Imani asked for the seventh time, chewing her lower lip nervously.

"I *promise*," Brock answered, rolling his eyes. "and Peter isn't *that* crazy these days. Remember how he's on our team?"

The two American Zodiac Heroes stood in the chill San Francisco evening outside a warehouse that had been garishly painted with scenes of demons and zombies and other nightmarish figures. A gust of wind whispered by them, playfully tugging at their heavy coats. It was Halloween night, and Brock had finally relented on

Imani's insistence that they needed to get out and have some fun. Life had been far too serious for far too long. In Imani's mind, their whole team needed desperately to get some happiness in their lives before they all went as crazy as Peter. Brock didn't disagree.

Ever since the visit from the goddess Libra and the Chinese Zodiac Hero of Dog just two short weeks ago, Brock had split his time between American Zodiac team meetings to discuss strategy with all of their new information, while simultaneously amping up the training regiment for Imani. He had even been bringing in other Heroes to give her personal guidance in different aspects of what it meant to carry the power of a god inside of you.

Maddy, Hero of Aries, had given Imani a stern lecture on the importance of control.

Barin, Hero of Taurus, had taught her the basics of how to put up mental barriers as a defense against those with telepathic abilities.

The Gemini Twins, along with Brock, had gone on and on about the importance of balance, not only in how you fought, but in life itself.

The Pisces men had spent most of their time flirting with her. So far, Imani had liked that practice session best.

And finally, on Halloween night, Imani's somewhat overbearing mentor had agreed to take her out to a haunted house, and now he was telling her that she was still expected to learn from it and not just have a good time! Which was what had made Imani suspicious about the whole set up.

Imani sighed, blowing an errant strand of brown hair out of her face, still not taking a single step closer to the front doors of the haunted house. The entrance had been made over to look like a giant, gaping mouth with glistening fangs thanks to a lot of plywood and some very adventurous artists.

Brock took Imani by the shoulders and turned her toward him. Although he stood just two inches taller than her at 5'8", he seemed so much bigger. For one thing, Brock had a body that was filled out and thick with muscle, like all of the male demigods of their Zodiac. Imani was thin to the point of being waifish, and ever since her mother...

"I promise," Brock said again, cutting off her inner diatribe before it had a chance to gain traction within her. "This is all about control. Your innate ability has to do in some part with fear, and so

99

here we are at a normal haunted house to see what might happen. All I'm asking is for you to hold on to that fear, and keep one eye turned inward to see if something sparks. You've already shown so much power through your shadow manipulation. Now I'm going to ask even more of you in an effort to dig deeper. I want to make sure that when everything comes to a head with the Dragon god and his nutso followers that you have every possible advantage available to you. You think I'm just going to train you half-assed and throw you to the wolves?"

Imani cocked her head and gave him a shy smile, liquid brown eyes sparkling mischievously. "Yes *sir*, Libra Hero *sir*! So, what did you do in the army when you were my age?"

Brock barked out a laugh, seemingly unfazed at her turn of the conversation. He should never have let slip to her what he used to do before going public with his Hero identity. She would find out eventually, of course. Imani was tenacious like that. "Tell you what, you discover a new power within yourself tonight, I'll tell you a few stories later. Deal?"

Imani grinned, nervousness falling away, and stuck her hand out. "Deal!"

Unseen by the two demigods as they strolled arm in arm through the giant plywood mouth entrance, a short, twitchy man who had been standing watch on the roof above raised a short-wave walkie talkie to his mouth. Moonlight glinted off of yellow teeth that had been filed down to razor points.

The Lobby

Like with any good haunted attraction, the fun started in the lobby, so that standing in line wasn't nearly as boring for the masses of people waiting to go into the haunted house proper. Different haunted attractions had different themes for their lobbies: some had ostentatiously costumed actors moving up and down the lines of people in a slow shuffling gait, moving in for a quick scare with younger kids, or posing for the cameras as adults giggled nervously and pretended that they weren't shaking with fear.

Other haunted houses, like the one Brock and Imani were so intent on entering, went all out right from the get go. This place, named *The Hellmouth*, had a raised dais set up behind crushed velvet ropes, with companies of dancers performing impressive renditions

100

of classic Halloween songs. The music was loud, pulsating thickly on the bass beats, and the dancers threw themselves into the performance with reckless abandon, feeding off of the energy of the crowds much like the vampires they were dressed up like.

Mentor and mentee moved slowly as the line inched ever closer to the entrance. The current song ended and the vampiric dancers on the dais were replaced with costumed ghouls who immediately launched into an energetic version of *Thriller*, complete with an over abundance of gyrating hips, much to the delight of the crowd. Imani had a death grip on Brock's arm and squeezed him almost painfully every time a 'ghoul' got too close, or a vampire hissed at her. Her excited squeals were a high pitched counterpoint to the moaning of the 'undead' actors.

Brock had put on a smiling face for the evening, but inside he was filled with turmoil. Not for the first time, he wondered if this was actually a good idea. Imani was the youngest of the American Zodiac Heroes, and as yet remained untested in a real fight. If something pushed her over the edge while in the haunted house, it could get dangerous *very* fast.

Stop it, Brock told himself firmly, not for the first time. *That's why you're here, genius. Imani needs this kind of exposure, and thanks to all the training, you know you can probably contain her if something happens. Now calm down and try to enjoy yourself a little. What could happen?*

Even as those last fateful words passed through his mind like smoke, memories of Andy, the Leo Hero, surfaced. Memories of how even the strongest of them could be brutally cut down in an instant. Brock shoved those thoughts aside with a grimace and stepped up to the inner entrance of *The Hellmouth* with Imani clinging tightly to him. The door before them swung open slooooowly, accompanied by a shriek of rusty hinges.

They stepped through into Stygian darkness.

Into The Hellmouth...

Right from that first step, something felt very, very wrong.

Brock and Imani, with their vastly different abilities, sensed it in different ways. To Brock, he felt an unnatural force pushing at the natural balance of the world around him. The psychic scales within his mind registered something abnormally twisted pulling down on one side, threatening...*everything.*

Imani, who was herself a combination of light and shadow right down her core, sensed all of the light around her fading. Not physical light; the haunted house attendants had done away with most of that already for the attraction. No, this was psychic light: the pure good of the people walking through the haunted house, actors included. A whirlpool had opened up, and all of that goodness was just draining away. A pervasive feeling of dread, of true fear, began to spread through the haunted house like psychic fog: unavoidable.

Inescapable.

Imani spun around, reaching for the swinging door they had just come through even as it slammed shut. A *click* sounded on the other side as the lock slammed home. That was when the screaming began.

Brock grabbed her shoulder, fingers tightening painfully. Imani turned fear-filled eyes toward him. "What's happening? Please tell me this is on purpose!" she yelled in his face as the screaming behind that locked door went on and on.

"Listen to me," Brock said in a too-calm voice. "I don't know what's happening, but we're going to be fine. Whatever's going on, you're ready. Ok? *You're ready.* Now the first thing we need to do is get out of here, because our presence is putting these people in danger. You can damn sure bet this attack is aimed at us. You with me?"

Imani nodded her head weakly. She reached up, pulled a scrunchie from her left wrist, and deftly wrapped her hair up in a bun so it wouldn't obscure her vision in a fight.

"I lead, you follow," Brock continued, glancing down the dark corridor they were standing in. He mentally visualized the layout of this place that he'd memorized earlier. *The Hellmouth* was separated into four different zones: swamp, mental hospital, zombie graveyard, and, last but not least, clown insane asylum. There *had* to be a staff exit somewhere! "You see better in the dark than I do, so keep your eyes open for a side door out of here."

A sickening *thump* hit the wall of the hallway ahead of them. Out of the darkness, a vague shape resolved itself into a person, one of the staff members who had dressed up as some kind of swamp creature. It stumbled toward them, a low keening sound issuing forth from a jagged hole in its throat. Shadows wreathed its face. As the unfortunate soul got closer, Imani saw with eyes that could pierce the shadows and nearly threw up.

102

The actor, most likely a girl if those long nails were any indication, had clawed a hole in her *own throat*. Suddenly, the shadows that had been swirling around her face dissipated, retreating back down the corridor and vanishing around the corner. The girl fell to the ground as if she had been on marionette strings that had just been cut.

"Brock," Imani whispered, fighting the scream that was trying to force its way out of her. "did you see-"

"Let's go," Brock said roughly, cutting her off and pulling her down the hallway. He didn't even look down as he stepped over the actor's body even as blood slowly pooled around the poor girl's head.

The two demigods turned a corner into the haunted swamp and were immediately assaulted by the sounds and smells of death. A coppery, metallic tang filled the air and laid siege to their nostrils. It was the smell of fresh blood, and it was *everywhere*.

The darkness of the haunted house was a blessing to Brock, as it obscured much of the gore around him. But to Imani, who could pierce shadows with her semi-divine eyes and see everything revealed in all of its intimate details, she found herself stumbling through a scene worse than any nightmare.

The 'swamp' was in reality a broad kiddy pool filled with murky water and fake seaweed in a large open square space that had been surrounded by wooden walkways. Each of the far walls had been liberally covered in green and brown crepe paper to simulate a jungle background, with a multitude of fake trees spaced out to provide depth and make the room appear bigger than it actually was. With the ever-present strobe lights pulsing at half speed, it made for a fairly realistic effect. Somewhere in the back of his mind, Brock applauded the creativity that had gone into the set up.

The actors had taken up positions in the swamp pool and around the walkways in the darkness, ready to jump out and scare people. Only it seemed now that every single actor had taken his or her own life in the time it took Brock and Imani to arrive, many of them using their own fingers to tear out eyes or claw through necks.

The music still pumped loudly through the open room, and the strobe lights continued to flicker fitfully, but nothing else moved.

"Who could have done this?" Imani whispered, eyes as wide as dinner plates.

Brock fought down his own hysteria. "Dragon," he whispered back. "The Dragon god's here. I can *feel* him."

103

A ripple appeared in the middle of the swamp water. Imani and Brock stood transfixed, staring as it moved outward, terrified of what it represented.

One of the bodies moved, climbing to its feet in jerky, unnatural movements of arms and legs that were already stiffening with rigor mortis. The actor appeared to be a young man in his early 20's, with a tight fitting black outfit and white makeup smeared on his clean-shaven face. Before his untimely death, he was probably some kind of swamp ghoul, or even a 'floater' that moved between the different rooms and scared people by leaping out of dark corners.

Two dark pits stared out at them where his eyes should have been. Blood glistened wetly on his cheeks. The corners of his mouth suddenly wrenched themselves up in a grimace that almost looked like a smile, baring his teeth.

"I know you," a voice croaked out from the actor's throat. The voice was too deep and grating to be human. Shadows whirled around the actor's head before swirling down and driving thickly into the empty eye sockets. That eyeless gaze was centered on Brock.

Imani felt Brock's body tense up as he stared down the terrible apparition in front of them.

"I *know* you," the voice issued forth again, confident and terrible. It sounded like two boulders being ground together and it made Brock's nerves stand on end. The dead actor opened his mouth to laugh, and water poured out and down his chest. "I saw you through the eyes of Dog's vessel, and then again through mine own disciple, the vessel of Rat. You are the one who is destined to bring me down? *You?*" The dead face sneered at them.

"Run," Brock whispered, so quietly that Imani could barely hear him. "For the love of our gods, *run.*"

"I'm going to kill you," the impossibly deep voice continued. One of his hands suddenly jerked up, pointing at Brock. "I'm going to eat your heart right out of your chest. And then I'm going to kill *her.*" The hand jerked to the side, pointing straight at Imani, and she felt something stirring within her. Something powerful. Something *dark.*

"Please," Brock gasped out, pushing with all of his strength at the overwhelming power rolling off of the body that the Dragon god was using. "Please, we can help you. Dog told us everything, how you just want a new world for yourself, a world where dragons-"

104

"YOU KNOW NOTHING!" the dead actor shrieked. Brock felt pure terror connecting him to the shadow god like an electrical conduit, pushing aside his meager balancing ability like it was nothing. He felt himself coming apart at the seams, his very soul shaking itself to pieces...

...and then, just like that, it was over. The terror was gone. No, not gone, just...shifted. It was at that moment that Imani took a step forward and put a hand on Brock's shoulder. He turned...and gasped.

Imani's eyes, normally dark brown, had turned as black as the shadows she manipulated. Brock could feel the fear that Dragon was radiating out, but more distantly now, like something just on the edge of his peripheral vision that was felt more than seen.

Imani smiled at him, and there was something sad about that smile. Something that spoke of acceptance to what can't be changed. She suddenly seemed much older.

"Rat is in the lobby. They need you."

"But-"

Imani put a finger against his lips, cutting him off. "I can do this. You have to trust me. This is what the training was for, right?" And then she grabbed him with inhuman strength and hurled him bodily back the way they had come.

Even as Brock's body was flying through the air, Imani was turning back to the dead actor carrying the Dragon god's spirit. When she spoke, the power of her goddess carried through her words, booming throughout the large room. **"It's not him destined to bring your downfall, you pitiful excuse for a god. It's me!"**

Shadows condensed and hardened around her body, wreathing her in darkness. At the core of her was all of the fear that she felt: fear of the Dragon god, fear for Brock, fear for herself, fear for all of the innocent bystanders, and it was all smashed down into a tight little ball within her. Imani grabbed hold of her shadows in one hand and her fear in the other and drove them together in a clap of thunder that rebounded throughout the room.

Darkness exploded out of her, throwing bodies through the air and vaporizing most of the swamp set. The body that the Dragon god had been puppeteering was shredded by her onslaught, and the Dragon god's spirit was driven forth.

In a single flash of insight brought on by her shadows touching the Dragon god's spirit, Imani suddenly understood that *he*

105

wasn't really here. The god was broadcasting himself somehow, like a radio signal that was using other people's bodies as receivers. The Dragon god had the ability to body jump, so he couldn't be nailed down, but he also didn't have full access to his own power. He was trying to use fear to paralyze, then move in for the kill. The Dragon god had made himself a spider at the center of a web of fear.

But fear was *her* power.

Imani took off at a dead sprint through where the kiddy pool had been, feet splashing through puddles of water and blood, allowing herself to think about how many people had to have been slaughtered, allowing the fear to rush through her veins and quicken her step. Then Imani reached inside herself, into that bubble of fear, and pushed it out of her body into a psychic shield that encompassed her from head to foot.

The Hero of Scorpio passed from the swamp section into a mental hospital wing and dropped down to her knees in a power slide that took her under the swing of an axe. The possessed actor gave a howl of rage, but Imani didn't even think, just bounced back up to her feet and kept running. Her head whipped back and forth as she searched for an exit.

The bloody set of the mental hospital gave way to a spooky graveyard with actors standing around uncertainly. The Dragon god's wrath hadn't reached this far into the haunted house yet, and thanks to the acoustics of the building, the actor's weren't sure whether the explosion and the screams were real or not. Many of them looked to Imani with hopeful eyes as she burst onto their set. Hope flashed to fear as they caught sight of the possessed actor with eyes wreathed in shadows that chased after Imani with an all-too-real axe clenched in broad hands, howling wordlessly.

Most of the actors dressed up as zombies scattered, but a few of the braver ones tried to get between Imani and the axe-wielder, recognizing a damsel in distress when they saw one. They died for their bravery, some by cruel axe swings that took off their heads, some by psychic blasts of the Dragon god's fear that induced mindless suicidal tendencies.

It gave Imani enough time to make her way past the graveyard and into the clown insane asylum, which consisted of a tight corridor that opened up on either side into rooms that had been outfitted to look like scenes from your worst nightmares.

Her heart beat an irregular staccato rhythm in her chest as Imani raced down the tight corridor. Above her head, strobe lights pulsed, splashing her shadow on the walls around her almost in time with her-

Movement!

Barely registering the attack in her conscious mind, Imani gave herself over to her newly trained instincts and threw herself flat. She heard a rush of air as something passed swiftly over her, smashing into the far wall. It was the axe from the possessed actor behind her, and it was dripping with blood and bits of skull.

Bounding back up to her feet, the 19-year-old demigod continued her headlong rush without looking back. A blood-streaked door appeared on her left and Imani dropped her shoulder down, reaching deep into her reservoir of power within her core. Her shoulder flashed black as shadows hardened around her, and she smashed through the door and into an inferno. A scream bubbled up to her lips as living flames reached for her with open arms.

Imani found herself in a room painted with incredibly realistic fire, thick brush strokes of orange and red and yellow, meant to simulate a working crematorium. The actor in this room, a thin-shouldered boy who looked about her age, was dressed up in a costume that appeared to be melted flesh.

"Who-" he began, then cut off as shadows exploded through the doorway and wrapped themselves around him like a cocoon.

Imani's anger burned hot, hotter than her fear, so hot it felt as if it would burn her from the inside out. She screamed and thrust a hand out to one side. At her mental command, black shadows from the corridor behind her streamed into the room and around her hand, lengthening and hardening until Imani held a midnight-black spear. With a roar of triumph, she plunged it into the cocoon of darkness and was rewarded with a mental scream as the darkness fled and the boy's body dropped to the ground.

Not sticking around to see if the boy was alive or dead, Imani whirled around on one heel and raced back out of the room and resumed her headlong sprint.

Another fifty feet of corridor disappeared beneath her pounding feet, and then suddenly she was bursting through the exit, the cool night air instantly freezing the sweat on her face and sharpening her already heightened senses.

The street in front of her was empty.

The screaming that had been coming from the lobby had stopped.

The night around her was coalescing into the outline of something so massive it denied comprehension. Something with wings.

"*I DEFY YOU, DRAGON!*" Imani screamed out, arms outstretched, shadows pouring into her hands and hardening into swords. She knew, instinctively, that she had one shot at this. She didn't know if she could kill him, but she could do something. She *had* to.

Imani prayed it would be enough.

The Dragon-shape before her stretched out its wings of pure darkness, opened up a mouthful of teeth the size of tree trunks.

As if in answer to her prayer, a hand dropped heavily onto her shoulder. Without moving a muscle, Imani knew it was Brock. Through her rapidly developing psychic abilities she could sense that he had been hurt badly, but he had still come back to her.

"You can do this," Brock croaked out, voice weak and full of pain. He squeezed her shoulder...and Imani felt pure balance flooding into her with his touch. Her fatigue was instantly washed away, and strength firmed her muscles.

Simultaneously, the Dragon-shape before her diminished in size.

Imani crouched down on legs that felt like pistons, bunching herself down as tight as a coiled spring, then shot straight up twenty feet into the air, a sword of hardened shadow held clenched in each hand. The Dragon god, once appearing to be as big as the sky itself, was rapidly shrinking down.

A single expression flashed through the Dragon god's eyes before she drove her swords through them.

Fear.

An excerpt from the diary of Imani, Hero of Scorpio

11/1/15

It's just past midnight, and I can't sleep. I kinda wonder when I'll be able to sleep again. After mom died, I had to start popping ambien at night not only to get to sleep, but so that I could sleep without dreaming of her. Just a month ago I finally stopped needing to take pills to get to sleep (I still dream of mom every night, but now it's sort of a comfort).

Right after I stabbed the Dragon god right through his gods dammed eyes, all I felt was adrenaline. I couldn't stop thinking about the new things that I learned to do with my power tonight! I've become a seriously powerful badass!

But the adrenaline faded, and now all I can think about are the people that died tonight just so the Dragon god could take a shot at us. I close my eyes and see the dead people that the Dragon god used like puppets. I've already thrown up twice since I got home. Dad thinks I'm drunk or something. Ha. If he only knew.

I don't know how to deal with this. So you know what, diary? I'm going to get my trusty ambien.

Goodnight.

CHAPTER 9

SAGITTARIUS

Sagittarius is a complex sign, a bridge between the human and the animal world, depicted as a centaur. The Sagittarian god, spanning these two worlds over the course of millennia, has slowly lost his grasp on humanity. The resulting madness has been passed on to his Heroes, with varied results. But one thing has always been constant: despite the madness, Sagittarian Heroes have always been good guys.

7:00 PM PST, November 26, 2015

Thanksgiving day. An auspicious day, filled with a very unique kind of power. The kind of power that brought people together, when differences were put aside in favor of the greater good.

At least, Ariele hoped that was the case.

The American Zodiac Heroes had gathered in a small, underground dive bar on the east side of San Francisco. They had reserved it for the night, which hadn't been too difficult considering who they were and what they represented. Despite the somewhat shabby appearance of the bar from the street, inside it was well lit and cozy. A dozen round, heavy wooden tables, well worn from regular use, had been haphazardly arranged throughout the dimly lit interior opposite the long, rectangular bar counter. In the far corner of the establishment, ping pong tables had been set up for beer pong on the right, vying for attention with the skee ball tables on the left. Incense sticks placed strategically about the bar drove away the bitter scent of old cigarette butts, from days before the bar had become a No Smoking Establishment.

The Hero of Virgo, seated at a folding table on a small raised stage sandwiched between the beer pong and skee ball, looked out at the other Heroes seated before her, most of them with beers in hand, thinking back to just a few months ago when she had first stood before them. Ariele had stepped into a role of leadership before having met most of her fellow demigods, and the experience had terrified her even as it made her stronger. Before, Ariele had felt beyond daunted at the charge of taking command of a group of super-powered strangers.

Now, a short time later and in the middle of a raging war with no end yet in sight, Ariele found herself looking at people she was

111

coming to know, people she already trusted with her life, and not just because she had to. She trusted them because they were heroes, not just Heroes.

All of them.

Clearing her throat nervously, Ariele looked at the front row, where the Heroes of Sagittarius and Gemini were sitting. No one had taken the seats on either side of them. Karina and Ivy, the Twins, both had looks of concentration on their faces. Crazy Peter, the Sagittarian, gave her a slight nod and a crooked smile that didn't reach all the way up to his unblinking eyes.

Trying not to over think what she was planning to say, the tall blonde launched right into it. "You all know me by now. We've worked together for a few months, and during that time I've gotten to know each of you beyond what powers you have, and what you can do on a battlefield. You've given me your trust, and I am eternally grateful for that. But I worry that you don't all trust each other yet, and that has to change. We're all fighting on the same side, and if we don't trust each other, how can we possibly fight together?

"I've called you all here today to share some new information that Peter and I have put together. And with the idea of trust and friendship in mind, I've asked Peter to be the one to share that information with you.

"Some of you have fought alongside Peter. Most of you haven't. But *all* of you know the rumors about him. Unfortunately, this has led to a lack of trust in some of you. Don't bother to deny it, to yourselves but especially to me. I see straight through you to the truth.

"All I'm asking is that you give him the same thing you gave me: a chance."

With that said, Ariele walked off the stage and sat down in the empty seat next to Ivy.

Peter popped up from his chair like a human cork out of a champagne bottle and sauntered up onto the stage, ignoring the table and standing tall, trying to exude a confidence that he didn't truly feel. His inner feelings were betrayed by the white-knuckled grip he had on his beer bottle.

Ivy and Karina followed him up and sat down at the table behind him, showing their support and lending more than a little credibility to what he was about to say.

Peter, at 6'1", was one of the tallest of the American Heroes, and appeared even bigger thanks to his muscular build. He had a wild tangle of curly brown hair that stuck up in every direction and added a couple inches to his height, and a beard that he only bothered to trim every few months, both of which seemed to reflect the madness within his mind. But in spite of his madness, he was one of the nicest Heroes on the team.

Peter was still a wreck after the death of his best friend Andy at the hands of the Monkey god. Since then he had only spent any serious amounts of time with Ivy, and due to that, the people staring up at him seemed more like strangers than teammates. Even Barin, the stalwart Hero of Taurus whom Peter had started to think of as his friend, now glanced away uncomfortably when Peter looked to him for support.

The somewhat crazed Hero took a slow, deep breath to calm himself. Ivy had a firm Pull on his sanity, ensuring that he'd hopefully be able to get through this meeting without an excess of giggling, wandering off on random tangents of thought, or raising his voice.

"I have two things to talk about," Peter said, his naturally booming voice echoing through the cavern-like bar. "First off, the rumors. I *am* crazy. Let's just get that out there. You all know it. Maddy, you know it better than most, as I absorbed *your* madness when the whole damn war started earlier this year."

The young flame-haired Hero of Aries grinned and gave him the thumbs up. Maddy was the only other Hero who understood what it felt like to be caught in the grips of madness, with no sense of control.

"It's obvious that most of you don't really trust me. I honestly don't blame you. If I was in your shoes, I'd probably feel the same. After all, a crazy person is a wild card. What I need you all to understand is that the state of my mind has never, and will never, affect who I truly am."

"Yeah?" Eli, Hero of Aquarius, barked out sharply from the table he was sharing with the Cancer men. Eli was Edgar's younger brother and, like Ariele, had only recently started meeting his fellow demigods. "and who *are* you?"

"One of the good guys," Peter replied quietly, staring Eli down. The Aquarian Hero looked away, unconvinced, and muttered something under his breath to Edgar and Alex. Edgar nodded, eyes locked on Peter with an inscrutable expression on his face.

"Look, you all want to understand my madness? The first thing is this: insanity isn't a state of mind, it's a *place*. It's everything in the universe that slipped between the cracks. There is no logic in this place, no rhyme or reason, no explanations. This place is vast, and at its core it is pure, uncontrollable, *primal* energy. And it is powerful beyond all belief.

"Maddy, when you meditate during your month of power, you hold that power at bay with your own inner strength. But last time, during the first Chinese Zodiac attack when you lost control, what did it feel like?"

"A tidal wave of rage," Maddy replied without hesitation. "It swept me away completely. I wanted to destroy everything."

"And without outside help, you would have. That rage you felt was just a small sliver of insanity, mindless and insatiable."

Edgar spoke up, asking a question that Peter was waiting for. "How were you able to take it away?"

Peter shrugged his shoulders. "Because I'm a direct conduit to the place that it came from. Like calls to like. I called to the madness inside of Maddy, opened myself up to it, and it came to me."

"You seem pretty normal right now," Sally, Hero of Capricorn, called out. Sally was sitting with Brock and Imani at one of the rear tables closest to the bar counter. Brock and Sally were working on their third round of IPA's, while Imani was sullenly nursing a root beer. Brock had forbidden her to drink any alcohol at the meeting because, while she was a demigod, she was still underage.

Peter smiled. Sally was one of his only real friends on the team besides the Gemini Twins. Sally knew *exactly* why he was normal right now, but she also knew that no one else did. Hence, the prompt for an explanation that would help the other Heroes really understand. That was the plan, at least.

"That," Peter said, looking back at Ivy. "is thanks to the beautiful Gemini Twin seated behind me." Ivy blushed and grinned, giving a little wave to the audience.

Turning back to the crowd, Peter went on. "First, I want you to picture a sphere. That sphere represents sanity, like a little planet where everything makes sense and adds up properly. On this planet, 2 plus 2 equals 4, right? Now, when you all got your full powers on your 18th birthdays, that sphere grew *exponentially* in order to deal with all of the new information that came flooding in along your divine conduit that leads back to your respective god or goddess. As

Heroes, we all have access to a much bigger portion of the universe than the average human does, and we need to be able to comprehend everything without, you know, our heads exploding. Basically our brains get real big while our heads stay the same size. Am I making sense?"

The Heroes nodded, several of them smiling at the silly analogy.

"As you all know thanks to our wonderful rumor mill, I got my full powers when I turned 13. The conduit to my god opened wide, but I was too young for my sphere of sanity to naturally expand and deal with what was happening. However, this didn't stop my *consciousness* from expanding. It had to, otherwise my head probably would have popped like a balloon. Literally. I think we take for granted exactly how much power we all have, and I'm not just talking about the sweet super powers, I'm talking about the portion of divinity that we take upon ourselves.

"Anyway, that original sphere you all have pictured so clearly in your somewhat divine minds? Imagine another sphere, much larger, drawn around the first one. The second sphere represents the size of my consciousness, same as all of yours. But my first sphere, my sanity, my ability to force things around me into logic and reason, never grew. My mind had to go somewhere, as I said, needed to find a different outlet to release the pent up pressure that was flooding my consciousness. My mind found refuge, if you can call it that, in a place that terrified me then and terrifies me now. A place *outside* of our rational universe."

Barin whistled softly. Eli and Edgar had identical shocked looks on their faces.

"Back to the reason why I appear to be so calm and collected and normal right now. Ivy, who you hopefully all look up to as she is one of our best and brightest, has the power to Pull, with a capital P. She is right now Pulling on my too-small sphere of sanity to expand it around my entire mind. And in answer to your next group question, no, she can't do it permanently.

"And hey, as long as we're acknowledging people, let's bring Karina into this!" Peter said as he spun and pointed out the other Gemini Twin. The look of concentration on her face had deepened, and sweat beaded on her furrowed brow. "Karina has the power to Push, again with a capital P. She is the reason why everything we say at this meeting is safe. She's maintaining a high level psychic Push around this entire bar to guard against eavesdroppers. You're all welcome."

Peter, feeling parched and suddenly remembering the beer bottle still clenched tightly in his right hand, took a long pull. The expensive pale ale, despite being lukewarm by now, had a refreshing effect on him, reminding him of his next point.

"There's one more thing I want to say about insanity, and how it's an actual place: *I'm not the only one connected to it.* The Dragon god of the Chinese Zodiac, our ancient and deadly adversary, is WAY crazier than I am. As in, several cards short of a full deck, not all the lights are on upstairs, batshit bonkers. While my own presence on that crazy plane of existence is mutable and, at times, tenuous, the Dragon god has himself *quite* the firm foothold. Over the last several months I've spent all of my free time searching that place, trying to find him so that we can at the very least get a better understanding of who we're going up against."

The bar was so silent you could have heard a pin drop.

"Last week I made contact."

As expected, Peter's teammates burst out into excited conversation, shattering the quiet like a grenade shattering fine china. Peter finished off his beer while he waited patiently for everyone to calm back down.

Finally, when the energized Heroes had managed to bring themselves under control, Peter went on, voice rising slightly to emphasize the importance of what he had to share.

"Everything, *from the beginning*, has been the Dragon god's plan. And we went right along with it again and again, inadvertently helping him achieve his goals."

Peter held up a hand, ticking off points on his fingers. "First, the Heroes of Dragon, Rat, and Ox attacked Maddy at her meditation house. Rat and Ox were there not to back up Dragon's Hero, but instead to ensure that he stayed long enough to get killed by an American Zodiac Hero so that the Dragon god himself could escape his mortal confines and be completely free and unfettered in our world."

Maddy looked down, ashamed, not wanting to meet the judgmental looks on the faces of her teammates around her.

Peter's voice rang out like a whip. "I don't want to hear a single word spoken out against Maddy! How the hell were any of us

116

supposed to know the true intentions of the Chinese Zodiac gods?! They're GODS, remember?!

"Moving on. Now the Dragon god was free, and he started enlisting, generally through force, other Chinese Zodiac Heroes to his side. You guys remember how Snake and Rabbit attacked Barin and Karina during the month of Taurus? Well, turns out they only attacked because the Dragon god sensed Karina trying to gather information about him. The Dragon god, being the 'master of shadows' type, didn't want us to glean a single bit of anything useful, so he sent Rabbit and Snake to curtail that attempt.

"In the month of Gemini, the Twins and I attempted an ambush of our own, in London. Needless to say, it, uh, didn't go so well. In the end, Gemini himself showed up to warn us of the Dragon god's *supposed* true plans: to free the rest of the Chinese Zodiac animal gods within our world. Unfortunately, that wasn't the Dragon god's endgame, just another feint. You *have* to understand, the only one the Dragon god truly cares about is himself. We've come to that realization late in the game, but hopefully not *too* late.

"Then, in the month of Cancer, the Hero of Monkey showed up to engage the Cancer men."

"Let me guess," Alex, the other Cancer Hero, quipped sarcastically as he leaned back his chair beside Edgar and Eli. "another feint?"

Peter barked out a laugh that carried no humor in it. "You bet your ass it was another feint. The Dragon god let the Monkey Hero off his leash simply to see what would happen! The following month, when the Monkey Hero went up against Andy and lost, which resulted in the Monkey Hero AND the Monkey god getting taken out, the Dragon god *exulted* in their deaths."

Brock, the Hero of Libra, raised his hand. When Peter gave him a nod, Brock stood up to formally address the stage. "I'm a little confused. I get what you're saying about the Dragon god needing to sacrifice his own Hero against one of us in order to break free into this world, but if all he wants is to break free of *this* world and find a new one, why continue to fight us at all? After all, when you get right down to it, he's a GOD, whereas we're all demigods. We shouldn't even be on his radar."

Peter smiled broadly. "An excellent point! The answer is almost ridiculous in its simplicity: limitation and uncertainty. While Dragon *is* a god, he weakened himself by coming fully into our world.

Remember the reason why he wants to find a new world: people don't believe in dragons in this one. That simple lack of belief makes him weak, and not nearly as powerful as he believes himself to be. The good news for us is that it means he can be beaten.

"As far as the Dragon god's uncertainty goes, look at the attacks that he's led himself. First, he sent his Hero to attack Maddy, fully expecting his Hero to be killed by an out of control demigoddess of war. Then he didn't *personally* surface again until less than a month ago at Halloween, and even *then* he didn't come in his own body, but rather projected a piece of his divine soul to body-snatch the unfortunate workers at the haunted house."

Imani, who was sitting next to her mentor, Brock, snapped at that comment. "He didn't just send a piece! If you had seen the size of him at the end when-"

"And how big was the Dragon god's spirit when Brock intervened?" Peter interrupted, not unkindly. "He shrank right down to a manageable size which allowed you to double tap him right through the eyes with your shadow swords. Which, if you don't mind my saying, is a particularly badass move and I'm sorry I wasn't there to see it."

Imani blushed, torn between pleasure at the compliment and embarrassment at the gentle rebuke.

"My point," Peter continued, beginning to pace up and down the small stage, "is that if the Dragon god had shown up in the flesh, so to speak, he wouldn't have been stopped so easily. It's my belief that the Dragon god wasn't so much trying to kill Imani as he was trying to snap her mind. I think he was making a power play to get her on his side. And that means he's afraid of her."

Brock didn't look convinced. He raised his hand again.

"I know I didn't fully answer your question," Peter said, looking at Brock. "So here's the rest: we're on the Dragon god's radar because he believes that someone in our group can help him tear open a hole to somewhere else."

"Who?" Maddy called out, sounding eager. But then, the Hero of Aries was always eager and spoiling for a fight.

"Here's where we enter the guesswork part of this little lecture series," Peter replied with a forced grin. "This whole thing started with Aries, who as you all know is in slot number one on our Zodiac wheel. I believe we will see an end to this, one way or another, with the last slot on the wheel." Peter pointed a finger straight at Max and Quinton, sitting side by side at a table near the back and somewhat removed from the other Heroes. "Pisces."

Everyone turned around to look at the young Pisces Heroes who suddenly looked like they'd rather be anywhere else but here in the spotlight of attention. Max cleared his throat. "Um. Why us exactly? Just because we're last?"

"There is power in the ending of a cycle," Peter answered slowly. "but it's not just that, I think. You two possess something within your powers that Ariele only just figured out recently while she was studying everyone. Something that you may not even know you have, consciously at least. Ariele, you want to cover this part?"

The tall blonde took the stage once more, and Peter gratefully sank into a seat between the Gemini Twins. Ivy reached over and squeezed his hand, giving him a smile, showing her support. Peter smiled back, though it felt a little strained. She had been Pulling on his sanity for a while now, and he felt his madness starting to push back. It was getting harder to keep his mind on point. He kept wanting to drift off and think about how *cool it is that because we're demigods, we for some reason all look like supermodels. I mean seriously, us guys look cut from the same beefcake cookie cutter, all big muscles and tight butts, and the every girl looks like she should be posing in-*

Peter shook his head violently and brought his attention back front and center, just in time to hear what Ariele was saying.

Ariele, meanwhile, looked at the two Pisces Heroes for a long beat before sweeping her gaze around all of the demigods seated in front of her. "The Dragon god needs the assistance of someone, or some*thing*, that stands in two worlds at once. By utilizing that duality in a moment of power, he could theoretically force a temporary bridge to another plane of existence, another world. At first I thought that meant that many of us were in danger. There is a duality to the powers of Gemini with the Twins, Sagittarius with the crossover of the human and animal worlds, and Capricorn with her hybrid animal of goat and fish. Aside from that, there are two Cancer Heroes, which creates its own duality. However, only one sign represents two entire *worlds*, and that is Pisces."

Quinton spoke up, looking confused. "I don't understand what you mean. Our powers balance light and darkness, but I wouldn't say that's two different worlds."

Ariele was shaking her head before Quinton finished talking. "Wrong. Your powers are a reflection of life and death itself. When you materialize your deathmasks, like Max did when he fought Rat in the initial attack against Maddy, you harness the very power of death itself. It is one of the greatest powers in the known universe, and it is why Rat ran so very fast to escape you, Max."

Rather than look proud, Max just looked troubled at her words.

"So..." Quinton said.

"Um..." Max added.

Peter jumped back up to his feet, coming around the table to stand next to Ariele. "Don't worry," he said with obvious false cheer. "you're two of the most dangerous dudes the world over. You're going to make *perfect* bait! The rest of us for the most part will continue with our current jobs. Cancer men, you're still on active patrol, with anyone else who wants to join you. The Gemini Twins will maintain a psychic connection between everyone."

Ariele stepped back into the spotlight smoothly as Max and Quinton were still sputtering. "When Peter said 'bait', he didn't mean we're just going to throw you both to the wolves. Most of us *will* need to keep a little distance to provide realism to the bait thing, but Eli will be staying with you as a kind of psychic bodyguard."

"I will?" Eli asked. The Hero of Aquarius was the most reclusive of the team of demigods, and he maintained his distance on purpose. Eli lived by himself in New York City, and the only Hero he maintained regular contact with was his brother Edgar, the younger of the two Cancer men.

Ariele smacked her forehead with her palm. "That's right, I completely forgot to ask! Um, would you mind playing bodyguard to Max and Quinton until we get this thing finished once and for all?"

Max and Quinton immediately began protesting that as two of the most dangerous dudes in the world, they naturally had no need for bodyguards. Eli didn't offer any verbal objections, but his raised eyebrows were a very loud statement.

Ariele embraced her natural abilities of command, drawing authority around her like a royal cloak, and froze everyone in their seats with a single glare. Max and Quinton broke off their arguing abruptly and had the decency to look repentant at their outburst.

"You want to know how Eli can help you both? He's the most powerful psychic we have. His 'better vibe' is so strong that he can disrupt the rage and insanity of Dragon. And I would think you two would jump at the chance to take advantage of the physical applications of his abilities, too, seeing as how you're both so wrapped up in the images of strength that you project." Ariele turned her attention back to Eli. "What do you say?"

Eli crossed thick arms across a barrel chest and nodded once, resigned. "I'm in."

"Good, I'm glad that's settled." Ariele said firmly, lowering her command power a notch so everyone could relax.

With the meeting coming to a close, the Heroes began splitting up into smaller groups to discuss some of the finer points of what they'd gone over. Max and Quinton drew Eli to the side and started trying to get to know this fellow Hero that they'd never had any contact with before.

Peter turned to Karina. The sweat that had been beading on her forehead was now dripping off of her chin. "Almost done, buddy, I promise! I just have to take care of one more thing that the Dragon god can't find out about."

Karina nodded, eyes tight.

Peter winked at Ivy, then hopped off the stage toward where his good friend Sally, Hero of Capricorn, was just climbing to her feet. Peter offered up his hand for a high five, which was enthusiastically returned.

"So," Sally said without preamble. "you said you had something you wanted to talk about after the meeting?"

Peter nodded. "I have an idea about a side mission to disrupt the Dragon god's plans even more. I talked it over with Ariele and the Twins, and they agreed it made sense. Here's the thing: I truly do believe we can take the Dragon god down. But I keep coming back to Brock's meeting with Dog and Libra, and how Dog loves the rest of his 'family', no matter how screwy they've all become. If we go into the final battle against the Dragon god and he brings some friends along, we simply can't guarantee that we'll be able to hold back and not kill them off."

"Sounds about right," Sally said with a thoughtful look on her face.

"So my idea is this: next month, on the cusp between our two months of power, we go do a little hunting of our own. We hit all of the Dragon god's known associates, that we can track down at least, and try to drive them off without killing them. That way, when we lure the Dragon god into attacking our Pisces guys in a few months, the Dragon god won't have any allies backing him up, and we won't have to worry about holding back!"

Sally pumped a fist in the air. "Good idea, I dig it! But how are we going to find the Dragon god's remaining allies?"

Peter grinned. "We go see a man about a horse!"

11/26/15

Good gods my head hurts. Whenever Ivy helps me out with the whole sanity thing, I feel great and normal and whatever *while* she's Pulling on my state of mind, but as soon as she stops, that conduit to crazy town seems to come back even stronger than before. I feel like I'm being stretched by one of those medieval torture devices between crazy town and the land of the sane.

With this war going on, sometimes I think to myself that maybe it would be better if I went down fighting in some glorious battle like Andy. He took out one of their gods, all by himself! And if I died, at least it would be an end to this constant battle for control in my own thrice-damned brain!

But then I think about Ivy. I haven't told her yet, but I love her. I mean I'm wildly, crazy, out of control in love with her! For Ivy, I choose to live. I'll put up with my timeshare apartment in crazy town for the rest of my life if I can spend that life with her.

We better win this war. I'm going to be seriously pissed if the Dragon god burns down the world when it's just started getting good.

CHAPTER 10

CAPRICORN

Capricorns, represented by the symbol of the goat-fish, are as dual-natured as their symbol. On the goat side, Capricorns are among the most ambitious of the astrological signs, always striving to climb the loftiest mountains, achieve the highest goals. On the fish side, Capricorns want nothing more than to relax, take it easy, live life in the most carefree manner. What is truly unique about those born under this sign is that they are able to find a perfect balance between ambition and relaxation.

1:50 PM PST, December 23, 2015

Sally stood in front of the bathroom mirror in the hotel she was staying at, pulling a brush through her long, light brown hair, straight with just a hint of a curl at the end. At least, it was light brown right now. It tended to change when she transformed, turning darker on one of her selves and lighter on the other. Sparkling blue eyes stared back at her from the mirror, and Sally smiled at herself, thinking yet again how incredibly lucky she was to be where she was. Yes, there was a war on. Yes, it was probably going to get worse before it got better. But she was a demigoddess! How many people are given the chance to save the world?

Sally looked herself up and down in the mirror, taking in her full curves, tanned skin, white teeth gleaming out of a stunning smile. Not only was she a demigoddess about to enter her *personal* month of power, but she was drop dead gorgeous, to boot. It was a good day to be alive!

That was Sally's daily mantra: it's a good day to be alive. Of the entire American Zodiac, Sally was the most unfailingly optimistic. When Andy died and Peter damn near fell apart at the seams, Sally was the one who helped Ivy comfort him and remind him that Andy was with his beloved Lindsay once more, pain free and happy in the afterlife of our Zodiac. And before that, when Maddy had killed the Hero of Dragon and touched off this whole war, the Hero had gone into a depression spiral, taking all of the blame on her own shoulders and briefly cutting off contact with the other members of the team. It was Sally who had been the one to stand firm by Maddy, reminding her repeatedly that in the heat of the moment, it was her or Dragon. There was no point rehashing the situation when Maddy had made the only decision that she could have! Sally didn't know it, but she was a beacon of light for the rest of the team, standing tall while the war threatened to pull them all under.

The slow rhythm of the brush pulling through her hair again and again had a hypnotic effect on Sally, and her eyes began to turn inward, racing through recent events. The hand pulling the hairbrush went into autopilot as Sally thought back to a few days ago, when a grinning Peter had shown up at her hotel with a tiny woman who appeared to be in her mid-70's. The woman's skin and accent proclaimed her to be an Aboriginal Australian, and that was all Sally needed to recognize her...

A few days ago...

"Horse?" Sally gasped out, a little afraid despite Peter's previous assurances that she would help them out. Her bright blue eyes widened as she stammered.

Peter, for once not smiling manically, looked down at the wizened woman standing next to him. "The Hero of Horse, to be exact."

Sally turned to her mildly unbalanced friend. "How did you even find her?"

Peter shrugged nonchalantly. "She's connected to a horse god, I'm connected to a centaur god, we've got stuff in common."

Sally raised an eyebrow.

A grin tugged at the corner of Peter's mouth. "Alright fine, the truth is *she* found *me*. The Hero of Horse is a clairvoyant. She sensed me, as well as my intentions, after the meeting we had last month. She searched me out, I explained our plan of driving off all of the Dragon god's allies, needlessly I might add because as I said she's a clairvoyant, and she said she wanted to meet you."

The Aborigine demigoddess stood there patiently while the American Zodiac Heroes discussed her as if she wasn't standing right there in front of them. Her eyes, a dark nut-brown, bored into Sally, making her more than a little uncomfortable.

Sally stood back and opened the door wide. "Um, please come in?"

Instead, the woman stepped up to Sally and reached her hands up, placing her palms lightly against Sally's cheeks. Sally felt a glow spreading through her mind, and a sense of calmness passed through her.

A long moment passed. The woman finally pulled her hands back, nodding to herself. "You will do. Both of you."

Sally was stunned. "How did you know there's two of me?"

The Hero of Horse suddenly smiled, and it lit up her whole face like a sunrise spreading across the sky. She tapped a finger against her temple and winked knowingly. "Clairvoyant."

Having completed her test, the woman finally deigned to walk into the hotel room, seating herself cross legged on the mattress. Sally and Peter pulled out cushioned armchairs and sat down to listen to the woman's story. She explained that the upcoming week marked the cusp between Sagittarius and Capricorn, and that it was known as the *cusp of prophecy*, a time when the two Heroes would be able to use their powers together to create great change in the world.

The Chinese Zodiac Heroes they needed to worry about, the ones that supported the Dragon god and would be at his side in the final battle if they weren't stopped, were all of those they had fought before: Rat, the cannibal. Ox, the destroyer. Tiger, the assassin. Rabbit, the sociopath. Snake, the poisoner. Rooster, the general.

Horse, being clairvoyant, didn't need to ask the American Zodiac Heroes for their promise not to kill her brethren. She did anyway. Peter and Sally solemnly swore that their only intention was to drive off or physically incapacitate the Chinese Zodiac Heroes, *not* kill them.

Then, and only then, did the Hero of Horse give them coordinates for the locations of the Chinese Zodiac Heroes. They were spread across three continents, but that wouldn't be a problem thanks to the Cancer men, who would apparently be providing escort.

The last thing the diminutive Hero of Horse said before she left was an apology to Peter. Despite being a demigoddess healer, she couldn't heal his madness. He brushed it off with a forced nonchalance, but Sally could tell he was bitterly disappointed under the casual facade.

The Present

Sally was startled out of her woolgathering by a knocking at her door. Her hand was still automatically pulling the brush through

127

her hair, which by now had achieved a silky gleam. She glanced at the clock.

2:00. Go time.

The demigoddess opened the door to admit two of her fellow Heroes, Peter and Edgar, both wearing the tightest black t-shirts they owned to show off their rippling physiques. If Sally didn't know any better, she'd swear they were related. The two muscular demigods even had a matching swagger and casual aloofness about the whole situation, despite the very obvious danger factor. Peter, in addition to wearing clothes so tight they may as well have been painted on, had a hard plastic case strapped to his back that held his self-proclaimed 'secret weapon'. Sally had laughed when he told her what he was bringing, but Peter had defensively replied that as the Hero of Sagittarius, he needed one to complete his image, and he couldn't just *create* one out of thin air while in human form.

Edgar left the door open behind him as he strolled into room a step behind Peter, hands thrust into the pockets of his blue jeans, which were as tight as his t-shirt. The Cancer Hero anticipated that they would be leaving extremely quickly and he didn't want to smash through it on their way out.

"Ready?" Peter asked, rubbing his hands together in anticipation, eyes darting around the room as if he expected an ambush in the hotel room. His tongue flicked out to lick his lips in a nervous gesture that Sally correctly guessed he wasn't even aware of.

Sally tossed her green brush down onto the tacky cream-colored bathroom counter. "As I'll ever be."

The three Heroes came together to stand in a semi-circle on the faded and stained hotel carpet, with Edgar at the center. The sideways speedster reached out and took a firm grip on the forearms of his friends and teammates.

"Remember," Peter said, cheek twitching slightly, eyes wide and unblinking. "we hit as hard and as fast as we can. These guys are equal to us in their own very different ways. If one of the other Chinese Zodiac Heroes gets forewarning about what we're doing, that could screw the pooch on the spot and send us home with no prize money before we even get a chance to hit the showcase showdown."

Sally rolled her eyes at Peter's poor analogy. "Dude, it's a good plan. Besides, we've got the whole 'cusp of prophecy' thing on our side, remember?" She felt power rushing through her veins, making her feel invincible. A little bit of caution was a good thing, sure, but they were ready for this. The Chinese Zodiac Heroes wouldn't know what hit them!

Peter took a deep breath. "Alright Edgar, let's do this."

Edgar smiled broadly through his beard. "You guys like Mexico?!" He tapped into his Cancer speed and the three would-be superheroes went rocketing sideways out of the hotel and out of San Francisco.

2:05 PM PST, Tijuana, Mexico

Edgar dropped them off outside the entrance of an underground gambling den in full daylight. Not that anyone paid much attention. In Tijuana, paying too much attention to something out of the ordinary was a good way to get shot. Or stabbed. Maybe both.

Edgar stayed outside to keep watch while Peter and Sally rushed in, ready to do battle with the forces of evil.

The steps leading down to the casino were old, wooden, and in ill repair. Neither Hero noticed. Peter was too busy unlimbering his bow and quiver from the plastic case on his back. Sally was too busy *splitting herself in two*.

Being the Hero of Capricorn, as represented by the goat-fish, Sally possessed the ability to divide herself in two, while still maintaining control over both selves with one mind. Her goat persona had increased strength and agility, and could climb anything as long as it had the tiniest sliver of an edge for her to cling to. Her fish persona could become incorporeal in order to 'swim' through solid objects. Given these abilities, Sally had named her two selves the Climber and the Swimmer, respectively.

The Climber lowered her shoulder and hit the basement door at an angle. The door exploded outward, sending a deadly hail of wood slivers at the gamblers crowded around the tables within. People of various nationalities, brought together by the shared experience of gambling large sums of money, much of it gotten through illicit channels, screamed and dove for cover.

Everyone except for Rat.

The emaciated Chinese Zodiac Hero with razor sharp teeth and fingernails stood staring dumbfounded as the two American Zodiac Heroes rushed in. Rat was wearing tattered black jeans and a multicolored poncho, neither of which looked like they'd been washed anytime this decade. A sliver of wood sliced along his cheek, which he barely noticed.

It wasn't until the Swimmer dropped through the floor in front of him that Rat finally realized he was being targeted. The villainous Hero turned to make a dash for the back exit, and tripped as the Swimmer's hand popped out of the floor at his feet and grabbed his ankle. Rat slammed face first into the hard packed dirt floor with a muffled curse.

Peter, arrow nocked and drawn back to his cheek, was keeping a wary eye on the crowd of people surging out of the back exit and up the stairs, on the off chance that someone tried to interfere.

The Swimmer, half of her body incorporeal under the ground beneath Rat, had taken hold of both of his ankles and held him tight, no matter how much he thrashed and cursed and kicked at her.

The Climber, wasting no time, strode rapidly over to the Chinese Zodiac Hero, bent down, and grabbed his wrists in a steel grip.

"Please," Rat whimpered piteously. "please don't kill me."

The Climber bent her head down close to scrawny cannibal. "Remember Aries?" Sally hissed. "How many of her people did you murder? How many of her people did you *eat?!*"

Rat saw the judgment in Sally's eyes and thrashed harder, trying desperately to free himself.

The Climber abruptly squeezed her hands tight, shattering Rat's wrist bones like toothpicks. Then Sally tore his hands right off.

Rat screamed loud enough to shake all of Mexico and parts of California.

The Swimmer drew herself out of the ground, merging back into the Climber. Sally, whole once more, spat on the Chinese Zodiac Hero bleeding on the ground in front of her. Peter nodded grimly, slowly easing the arrow in his bow, then replacing it in his quiver. The two American Zodiac Heroes left the casino as quickly as they'd entered it, rejoining Edgar topside.

"How'd it go?" Edgar asked conversationally as people ran every which way around them.

"I tore his hands off," Sally replied, eyes grim.

"Good!" Edgar exclaimed happily. "Who's next?"

Peter grabbed a piece of paper out of his back pocket. On it was a list of names and places. "We're off to Nigeria to pay Ox a visit. In between doing jobs for the Dragon god, it looks like he's set himself up as a dictator."

"Are we sure we don't want to get Barin involved for this one?" Sally asked. "He still has a grudge after the last time he and Ox got into it."

Peter shook his head firmly. "We don't want to kill Ox, and I don't think Barin could control himself."

Edgar stepped forward and took hold of his friends once more. "Hold onto your hats, ladies and gentlemen."

The world turned into a blur as they sped across the ocean towards the African continent.

10:42 PM WAT, Lagos, Nigeria

It was something of a shock passing from mid afternoon to full night in the blink of an eye, but the American Zodiac Heroes adjusted quickly. They were on the outskirts of the town, outside the military base that Ox had set himself up in.

Horse had given them a detailed layout of the place from her glimpse into the near future. Supposedly, Ox would be out on patrol with a regiment of guards tonight, in order to be seen and to spread his reign of terror. The Chinese Zodiac Hero was obsessed with appearing strong and in control, and to that end he personally executed a random person almost every night.

No wonder Barin despised him so much.

As soon as Edgar dropped them off, the Cancer Hero sped back out into the night for a swift perimeter check to make sure that Ox was on his way to his date with destiny. If the American Zodiac Heroes had planned this right, Peter and Sally could just sit tight and wait for Ox and his soldiers to come to them.

Deep in the shadows, Peter knelt down and drove all but one of his thirteen arrows into the dirt in front of him in a loose semi-circle. Then he readied his bow, nocking his last arrow but not drawing it back.

Sally split in half, becoming the Climber and the Swimmer, and took up flanking positions on either side of her friend. She stared through two sets of eyes at the military base in front of them. The base was *huge*, taking up a square block of land, and was surrounded on all sides by electric fences topped with razor wire. At each corner there was a squat guard tower with bright halogen lights that combed through the darkness. Sally and Peter were on a street, if it could be called that, just outside of the range of the lights.

"Remember," Sally said quietly, speaking through both the Climber and the Swimmer simultaneously. It was eerie to listen to. "You take the soldiers. Ox is mine."

Peter nodded. They had already discussed how to take down someone with super strength, especially without Barin to help them out. Sally's Climber might be strong, but she wasn't *that* strong. In the end, Sally's idea had been brilliant in its simplicity.

At that moment, Edgar came speeding back up to them. "Absolutely perfect timing," he pronounced. "Ox is on his way with ten soldiers."

"How many arrows do you have?" Sally asked Peter.

"Baker's dozen."

"Good. Give me two."

Without a word, Peter yanked two arrows up out of the ground and passed them over to the Climber. She held them loosely in her hands like a pair of daggers.

Edgar wished them luck before turning sideways and speeding off to provide backup should any more soldiers arrive.

Sally and Peter heard Ox and his soldiers coming before they saw them. The group came around a corner ahead of them, outside of the fence, apparently doing a perimeter check of their base before heading into the town to pick out a victim for tonight's execution.

Ox himself stood head and shoulders taller than any of his soldiers. All of the soldiers wore camouflaged fatigues with full body armor, but Ox strode about bare-chested, showing off his size as well as making a statement. The Chinese Zodiac Hero had no need of body armor, and he wanted people to know it.

Peter raised his bow, drawing the arrow back to his cheek. He waited patiently for the group to get just a little...bit...closer...

Peter loosed the shaft, hands working automatically to draw the next one from the ground before him. He had three arrows in the air before the first one had found its target in the throat of the soldier walking just to the left of Ox. Soldiers began falling one after the other, dropping like flies without a sound.

That was the basis of Peter's power. He never missed. Ever.

132

Less than ten seconds had passed since Peter had shot that first arrow. Less than ten seconds to take ten lives.

If Ox was scared, he didn't show it. He crossed tree trunk sized arms over his enormous chest and waited calmly with a smile on his face, overflowing with arrogance.   Sally didn't make him wait long.

The Climber and the Swimmer sprinted forward as one, covering the distance between her and Ox in ground eating strides. Behind her, Peter nocked his final arrow, covering Sally while trusting in her abilities.

The Climber dropped back a half step, letting the Swimmer reach Ox first. Ox swiftly uncrossed his arms and unleashed a powerful right jab that, had it connected, would have knocked Sally's head right off of her body.

The Swimmer turned incorporeal and allowed Ox's fist to pass through her head.

Sally's plan had been simple. Get Ox alone, rush him, get him off balance, and go in for the strike as quickly as possible. Ox might have super strength and unbreakable skin, but he had a weakness that could be exploited. He wasn't unbreakable everywhere, according to Horse. Time to put Horse's intel to the test.

The force of Ox's punch was enough to cause him to stumble forward a few inches. That one stumble was all it took.

The Climber darted in on sure feet, passed through the Swimmer, and rammed her two arrows straight into Ox's eyes. The gigantic dictator screamed even louder than Rat, a deep basso bellow that Sally and Peter felt in their bones. The soldiers back in the guard towers heard it, and immediately set off the alarms.

The Climber and the Swimmer merged back into one. "Barin says hi," Sally growled at the Chinese Zodiac Hero before turning and sprinting back to Peter. Edgar beat her there, grabbing hold of his teammates.

"London?" Sally asked.

Edgar shook his head. "Alex just got in touch with me while I was running the perimeter. Says that Horse made contact with our team in San Francisco and told us to take Tiger and Rooster off of our list for now. Didn't say why. Just that it needed to play out that way."

Peter pulled out his list. Behind them, Ox was still screaming and rolling around on the ground, clutching at the arrows sticking out of his ruined eyes, blood and gore covering his face like a gruesome mask. "Guess we're going to France, then. Let's pay a visit to Rabbit."

11:23 PM CET, Paris, France

Edgar dropped them off outside of what appeared to be a raging nightclub in the heart of downtown Paris before racing off into the night. He said something about Alex needing back up somewhere in Los Angeles, and that he would return as soon as he could.

Peter was eyeing the passing Parisians threateningly, completely on edge and barely hanging on to his sanity. Sally touched his shoulder and Peter spun around, eyes rolling wildly as he tried to look in every direction at once.

"Easy buddy," she said, voice pitched low. "Stay with me here. Remember the plan?"

Peter squeezed his eyes shut and took a deep breath. "I'll head in, stir up some trouble, try and draw Rabbit out."

"Right," the Capricorn Hero nodded. "I'll be out here, on the street in front of the entrance *and* on the roof to block his escape. *Don't forget about his legs!* This bastard could break either one of us in two with a single kick."

Peter grinned, eyes popping back open. "We'll see what the 'cusp of prophecy' has to say about that." Without another word, he spun and darted into the club, shoving people out of his way.

Sally sighed, popping her knuckles before dividing in two yet again. The Swimmer stayed standing right outside the entrance, as agreed upon. The Climber moved over to the side of the brightly lit, three story high building. Reaching up, she grabbed the edge of a brick and nimbly hauled herself upward, moving with grace and ease from brick to window ledge to drainage pipe. With her power, she could climb anything that had even so much as a *seam* disrupting its surface, and she never got tired.

The Climber was just cresting the edge of the rooftop when the sounds of a riot erupted from the club's entrance. The Swimmer watched nonplussed as partying Parisians began pouring out of the club and running off into the night. Somewhere in the club, glass shattered. Someone screamed.

Sally smiled with both of her mouths simultaneously. Peter might be a bit of a nutball, but he was damn good at causing chaos!

Speak of the devil. Peter came sprinting out of the club, laughing his head off. Rabbit, a wiry Frenchman nearly as tall as the Sagittarian Hero, was right on his heels, a snarl contorting his handsome features. The man was a complete sociopath who delighted in hurting other people. Peter's part of the plan had been to simply piss him off. The best way to take down a sociopath was to make them lose control.

In all the confusion, Rabbit didn't even notice Sally until the Swimmer stuck her foot out and tripped him as he went running by. Rabbit went sprawling. Peter immediately spun around and jumped on him.

Rabbit, quicker than any of the other Chinese Zodiac Heroes now that Monkey was dead, rolled away from Peter and bounced back up to his feet. Recognizing Sally for who she was, Rabbit knew he was outnumbered. The Frenchman bent down to the ground, bunching his powerful legs like pistons, and shot up into the sky like a human pinball.

The Climber was ready. She jumped off the roof just as Rabbit went rocketing by, grabbing him around the waist and forcibly bearing him back down to the ground. They hit the sidewalk hard enough to rattle their teeth. Even demigods had limits.

While Rabbit lay there dazed, Peter and the Swimmer walked up on either side of him. Rabbit looked up and opened his mouth. The curse on his lips turned into a shriek as Peter and the Swimmer stomped down on his kneecaps, shattering them both.

The Climber bent down and placed a hand on each broken kneecap. "I hear you like to hurt people," she said, voice dripping venom. She squeezed, much like she had squeezed Rat's hands off what seemed like a week ago now. Using her enhanced strength, she ground Rabbit's shattered knee bones together, grinding them into powder. Rabbit's eyes rolled back into his head and he passed out from the pain.

The Climber straightened up, then melded back together with the Swimmer.

Peter nodded with approval. "So as soon as Edgar gets back, we head to India to-"

"No," Sally said tiredly, shaking her head. "No more. I can't."

"But-"

"*NO*. I know what you're going to say, Peter. The freaking 'cusp of prophecy', and taking them out before they take us out, and they deserve it, etc. And yes, they do deserve it, I'm not arguing that. It's just," Sally threw her hands up in frustration. "we aren't *them*! We're better than them! We're supposed to be the *superheroes*! But look at what we've done tonight. I tore someone's hands off! I don't care if he had it coming, I don't care if he's a mass murderer who eats people, all I care about right now is that I have to live with the fact that *I tore someone's fucking hands off!*" Sally felt wetness on her cheeks and realized she was crying. "We're supposed to be the good guys," she whispered.

Peter put a hand on her shoulder. "You're right," he said softly. "Gods help us, you're right. I'm so, so sorry."

Edgar picked that moment to speed up to the scene. He took one look at his teammates, then at Rabbit lying unconscious at their feet. "Um...you won, right?" Sally turned away, swiping a hand furiously at her eyes.

Peter nodded. "Yeah, we won. If you can call it that." The Hero of Sagittarius had a bleak look in his eyes that Edgar hadn't seen before. "Forget it, let's go."

"Where to next?"

Sally turned back to her friends, eyes still glistening with tears. "Home," she said firmly. "Just take us home."

Excerpt from the diary of Sally, Hero of Capricorn

12/24/15
Christmas Eve morning. Never before have I felt less like
celebrating. I don't get it! Our mission started off so simply:
deliver some well-deserved vengeance to the bad guys. When I
think about it objectively, I agree with what me and Peter did! Rat
is a mass murderer and a cannibal, and he got his hands torn off,
hands that have taken so many lives before we got to him. Ox was
an evil dictator with super strength who couldn't be stopped, and
yeah, he was a mass murderer, too! So he lost his sight, and good
luck being an evil dictator when you're handicapped in such a
fashion. And lastly, Rabbit, that sociopath who has enjoyed
putting the hurt on people for the gods know how long. And he
lost his legs, which means he'll never be able to pull a quick escape
ever again.

I think about this and I think that they deserved it! An eye for an
eye! Score a few points for the good guys!

Except for one thing: *I'm* the one who tore a person's hands off.
I'm the one who stabbed someone in the eyes and blinded them
forever. *I'm* the one who turned someone's kneecaps into powder.
So what does that make me?

Am I still one of the good guys?

CHAPTER 11

AQUARIUS

Aquarius is the sign of the visionary, the odd man out in the zodiac wheel who is constantly looking to the future, rather than the present or the past. Aquarius never stops asking why. Aquarius never stops trying to make the world around them *better.*

3:11 PM EST, February 2, 2016

Eli, Hero of Aquarius, 6'2" and muscled like a human tank, took a very careful sip of his piping hot black coffee. The mug, which said *Age of Aquarius* on it, looked comically small in his large hands. Despite his care, a little coffee dribbled over the side of the mug and into his neatly trimmed brown beard. Eli sighed and, regardless of the fact that they were nowhere near him, blamed the Pisces Heroes.

Max and Quinton had been staying with Eli in his large yet spartanly furnished 2-bedroom apartment on the Upper West Side of New York City ever since Crazy Peter had made his pronouncement about using the two of them as bait. The apartment was enormous and easily held the three of them, but Eli still would have preferred having the space to himself. Aquarius Heroes weren't known for being overly sociable for extended periods of time.

Eli, at 30 years old, already held three PhDs, in math, physics, and theoretical medicine. That last category had been made up specifically for him. For years now he had been studying ways to try and reverse-engineer the godlike abilities of the chosen Heroes in order to make them accessible to the average populace (specifically, the enhanced healing that most of the Heroes took for granted). Eli's attempts hadn't been successful thus far, but he hadn't given up hope.

And now here he was, playing babysitter to a couple of demigods who were barely old enough to drink.

A slight tapping sound came from the large picture window set into the east wall of his bedroom, specially designed and custom installed to catch the sunrise and start his days off properly. Eli knew it would be his older brother Edgar before he even turned his head, and it had nothing to do with telepathy.

Edgar, Hero of Cancer and sideways speedster, was standing on Eli's fire escape with a grin on his face. Eli set his coffee mug down gently on a mahogany nightstand before getting up and strolling over to unlatch the window, allowing his windblown brother to hop down into the huge bedroom.

"Did you hear the news?" Edgar burst out eagerly before his feet had even hit the custom Berber carpet that Eli had had installed in each of the two bedrooms the year before.

Eli rolled his eyes (*I seem to be doing that a lot lately* he thought) and turned his back on his brother, walking over to retrieve his coffee. He preferred drinking coffee while it was still piping hot, and he wouldn't allow anyone or anything to keep him from enjoying it. "Of course not. Because you're all in San Francisco, and we've been sitting on our asses here in New York. Bored to tears, I might add."

Edgar cocked his head, grinning. "Where are the Pisces guys?"

As if awaiting a formal summons, Max and Quinton burst into Eli's bedroom without even a courtesy knock. Eli rolled his eyes. Again. The two young Heroes jumped at any chance to get away from the monotony of being bait, especially when it included hearing news from the rest of the team.

"Is it about Sally?" Max asked eagerly, rubbing his hands together with anticipation. Quinton threw himself down on Eli's king-size bed and started bouncing up and down. The Pisces Heroes, after hearing how Sally had put the hurt on all those bad guys last December, had pretty much started worshipping her, and had nicknamed her the 'Queen of Kicking Ass'.

The smile on Edgar's face faltered for a moment. "No," the Cancer Hero replied, shaking his head, unkempt brown hair swinging around his face. "She still won't talk to anyone about what happened. She's kinda torn up about what she did."

"But what she did was awesome!" Quinton protested, pumping his fists in the air and bouncing harder on Eli's bed. "Totally brutal!"

Eli whipped around, anger surging. The two Pisces Heroes immediately fell silent from the intense look on his face. Quinton stopped bouncing on the bed. "That's just it, it was 'totally brutal'!" Eli sneered at them, disgusted. "Sally was right when she said we're supposed to be the good guys. We can't go rushing around acting like the ends justify the means, or else we truly will be no different from the Chinese Zodiac 'Heroes'."

Max opened his mouth but no retort came out. Quinton looked away, face turning beet red with embarrassment.

Edgar jumped into the silence with a quick change of subject. "I have news about your whole situation here in New York! Just yesterday, when Ivy was doing a routine psychic sweep of the European continent trying to Pull information, she got a hit. In Moscow."

Eli's dark brown eyes narrowed. "Rooster?"

Edgar nodded excitedly. "Rooster *and* Tiger!"

Max and Quinton high fived, while Eli took a long, slow sip of his coffee while he processed this new information. Rooster and Tiger were among the most powerful and ruthless of the Chinese Zodiac Heroes, and they both had very personal motives for wanting the rest of them dead. Rooster was missing three fingers from his right hand as well as his left eye thanks to Ivy, and Tiger was still sore about the whole 'murdering his brother the Dragon Hero' issue, despite the fact that the Dragon god had orchestrated the whole thing from within.

Truth be told, Eli's biggest problem with the Pisces guys wasn't the fact that they were young, or even that they were somewhat untested in battle. His problem was their perspective. Max and Quinton thought that Sally had dealt a huge blow to the Chinese Zodiac Heroes last December by effectively removing Rat, Ox, and Rabbit from the equation. What they didn't realize is that those three were the dregs of the Chinese Zodiac. For hell's sake, Rat was nothing more than a slightly overpowered rodent of a man with filed teeth who spent his free time in Tijuana gambling in basements!

Now Rooster and Tiger were being drawn, *purposefully*, back into the fight. Max and Quinton weren't even scared.

They really, really should be.

"...only one problem," Edgar was saying, pacing back and forth across the gray carpet.

Eli realized he'd completely tuned out for the last minute as he had worked his mind around the issue of Rooster and Tiger. "What was that?" he interrupted.

Edgar cleared his throat. "I said, the bit of info that Ivy managed to Pull made it seem like the two Chinese Zodiac Heroes are aware that this is just a trap," he repeated.

"Well of *course* they'll know this is a trap," Eli said for what felt like the thousandth time, ever since this idea had been proposed. He threw up his hands in exasperation. "We may as well have hung a sign outside my apartment saying 'We're waiting for you, come get a piece'."

"We want so much more than a piece, boy," a voice hissed right behind Eli. The Hero of Aquarius spun around just in time to catch a solid right hook across the jaw that sent him flying across the room. Eli slammed into the wall and felt something in his shoulder break. His coffee mug went spinning off in a different direction, splashing black coffee all over the carpet and one of the walls.

Dazed, Eli pushed himself up off the floor with his good arm, shaking his head to clear his vision. Standing in the doorway, larger than life, was Tiger.

At 6'6", the Chinese Zodiac Hero from England loomed over the shorter American Zodiac Heroes. Camouflaged war paint was streaked at an angle down his face; as Eli stared in horror, the 'paint' rippled, colors changing, as Tiger's body automatically blended into his surroundings. Tiger's form fitting camo clothing acted in the same fashion. It was eye-wrenching to stare at him for too long, as parts of him seemed to vanish and then reappear. The illusion, added to his enhanced speed and strength, made him one of the deadliest Heroes of his current Zodiac roster. Hanging off of his belt in sheaths, close to either hand, were two long bladed knives *And he was in Eli's bedroom.*

Tiger stepped fluidly to one side, allowing Rooster to walk through the doorway and join the party. Rooster stood a couple inches shorter than Tiger, putting him about even with Eli, but he seemed to loom even larger. Maybe it was due to the fact that where Tiger was all lean, tight muscle, Rooster was thick, barrel-chested and had the look of a tavern brawler. The eye patch covering his ruined left eye socket made him look even more villainous.

Max and Quinton might have been young, but they weren't naive. All of their previous bravado vanished like fog burning away in the sun, and the Heroes stood side by side with fists raised in front of them, calm and collected and ready for a fight. Edgar stood a half pace behind them, body angled slightly to the side, ready to rush in.

Eli's mind worked through the problem in front of him, racing faster than ever before.

Edgar has super speed, but so does Tiger, at least to some extent. We never did learn who was faster, although I would put my money on Edgar. Max and Quinton can attempt to materialize their deathmasks, but in broad daylight who knows how effective they'll be. Rooster supposedly never tires, so if this fight is drawn out, they'll beat us down eventually and take us out. Physically speaking, they're stronger.

How can I make this better? Gotta buy some time.

Tiger locked eyes with Eli as he climbed to his feet, giving him a nod that seemed to convey respect. Of course, Eli had heard rumors that Tiger was old school. Give honor to an enemy when honor is due. Maybe he could use that. While he thought, Eli grabbed his broken shoulder with his good hand and pushed the bones back into place, then, with a focused burst of power, knitted the bone together, making himself *better*.

Rooster looked them over, studying them for a long beat. "Where is short redhead?" he asked finally, Russian accept thick on his tongue. "She owes eye to me." He reached up and fingered his eye patch.

"Go fuck yourself," Max spat out.

Tiger seemed to vanish. One moment he was standing next to Rooster, then suddenly he had Max by the throat and was lifting him into the air. "You show respect, *boy*," he said, English accent moderately easier to understand than Rooster's. "This is no game. You are all going to die this day, but depending on your attitude, that death might be little more drawn out than you would like."

Max gasped for breath. Quinton, rage burning in his eyes, shot a hand up to materialize his deathmask. Tiger didn't even look at him, just lashed out with his free hand and sent Quinton flying to the floor.

Edgar tensed, body starting to blur with pent up energy. This wasn't going to end well.

"Wait," Eli shouted, taking a step forward. Max's face was turning blue. "Please," Eli said, lowering his voice and pushing out with the psychic power he had nicknamed his 'better vibe'. "It doesn't need to go like this. You want answers? You talk to me. Just...put him down."

Tiger's painted face quirked up in a smile as he lowered Max down to the ground, then casually shoved him to the ground next to Quinton.

Eli pushed his better vibe out harder. If he could keep them off balance just long enough... "You want to know where the redhead is? Where the rest of our whole team is? Try San Francisco. We four are just here as bait."

Rooster nodded as if Eli was confirming his suspicions. "Da, this we know. Is terrible plan, because plan *worked*. Now we kill you, then go to San Francisco and kill rest."

"No, I don't think you will," Eli said quietly, fists clenched tightly by his side. "We know that your Dragon god needs these two to open a portal for him to a new world. That means they need to be kept alive. Unfortunately, we can't kill you, either. But we do have a very special prison all ready to go."

Tiger's eyes tightened and his mouth twitched, almost as if he was fighting back a smile. "What makes you think we're here to help the Dragon god? He's no god of mine."

Suddenly everything fell into place in Eli's mind. Tiger *knew* that the Dragon god had set up his brother to die so that the god could break free. Tiger and Rooster weren't on the Dragon god's payroll any longer, they were just here for their own revenge! They had no reason to leave *any* of them alive.

Eli felt a wave of fear course through him and angrily shoved it down. Now was not the time for fear. Now was the time for action.

Edgar glanced over, locking eyes with his brother. Eli heard Edgar's telepathic voice slip sideways into his mind. *--Thoughts?--*

--You need to get them out of here.--

--But what about you?--

--NOW, EDGAR!-- Eli's mental response lashed out hard enough that Edgar physically recoiled as if slapped.

Eli took a deep breath, then pushed out with his better vibe at the two Chinese Zodiac Heroes as hard as he could. Their minds were too dark for him to do more than confuse them for a split second as *good* thoughts blossomed around their urges to kill and get revenge, but a split second of distraction was enough.

Edgar reached down, grabbed hold of Quinton and Max. The three American Zodiac Heroes blurred as Edgar sped them all out of the picture window and out of New York. Leaving Eli alone to face down two of the most powerful Chinese Zodiac Heroes to ever walk this earth.

Eli popped his neck ostentatiously and rolled his shoulders. No innocent bystanders to worry about. No teammates to watch out for. His time to shine.

Tiger and Rooster watched the three American Zodiac Heroes make good their escape without trying to follow. They knew exactly where they would be heading. The Brit and Russian would be

144

following in short order, just as soon as they took care of one final detail.

"I truly hope you have more up your sleeve than that little head trick, mate," Tiger said in his cultured, British accent. Rooster grinned.

"Oh, I do," Eli replied calmly, staring them down. As if the three of them were having a casual conversation about the weather over a nice cup of tea. "See, I make things *better*. I honestly hoped that I could even reach the two of you, but as I'm sure you're both well aware, you're too far gone to ever get better. You're a metastasized tumor that needs to be cut away from humanity, so that the rest of us may flourish." Rooster's good eye narrowed at the insult. Tiger just laughed. "I can also make *myself* better," Eli finished quietly. The Hero of Aquarius turned on his power full force, focusing it inward.

Before the astonished eyes of the Chinese Zodiac Heroes, Eli started to grow. His expensive designer clothing stretched tight and then began to tear at the seams as Eli added another foot to his height. His muscles, bones, and tendons grew proportionately inside of his body. Eli's heart grew as well, beating faster and faster, pumping dangerous amounts of adrenaline through his supercharged veins.

Within seconds, Eli towered over the Chinese Zodiac Heroes at a solid 7'2". He cracked his neck again, and it sounded like a shotgun blast in the now much smaller seeming bedroom. *This* was why Eli had gotten an apartment with cavernous ceilings. Just in case.

Tiger moved first, as Eli anticipated he would. The six and a half foot tall Brit, with his enhanced speed and military training, was a front line fighter. In chess, Tiger would be the queen, moving in every direction and laying waste to the weaker pieces. Rooster was more like the king, slower to move but controlling the actions of the rest of the pieces on the board.

Eli, with his better vibe pulsing strongly within him, was now almost as fast as Tiger. He sidestepped the Brit, snapping out his elbow into where Tiger's face should have been. But this wasn't Tiger's first rodeo. Tiger dropped to his knees, flowed under Eli's attack, and delivered a swift punch to the side of Eli's left kneecap.

Eli felt his leg collapsing under him, but managed to get a grip on Tiger's arm as he fell. Spinning as he toppled forward, Eli

145

hurled the smaller Chinese Zodiac Hero at his teammate. Tiger smashed headfirst into Rooster's barrel chest, sending them both sliding out of the bedroom and into the spacious living room beyond.

Eli had just enough time to use his power to rearrange his kneecap and regain his feet before Tiger was rushing back in to the attack, long bladed knives tightly gripped in each hand. Those knives darted in almost too fast for Eli to track, despite his own enhanced speed. It was all he could do to keep Tiger from slicing open any major arteries. In a matter of moments, Eli was bleeding from half a dozen cuts on his arms and chest, and he didn't have the mental fortitude to maintain his size *and* heal himself simultaneously. Somewhere in the back of his mind, Eli irritably wondered how long it would take to get the bloodstains out of his expensive carpet.

The Hero of Aquarius gritted his teeth and dropped his left arm, feigning weakness. Tiger took the bait, springing forward for the kill, teeth bared like his animal namesake. At the last possible second, Eli reduced his size by a few inches, so that Tiger's blade pierced him in the shoulder instead of the heart. Teeth clenched against the pain, Eli wrapped his long, thick arms around Tiger's waist, keeping the Brit trapped against his chest.

Tiger's eyes grew wide as he struggled frantically to free himself.

"I can't kill you," Eli gasped out. "But try coming back from *this!*" The American Zodiac Hero squeezed his huge arms as tightly as he could and felt with grim satisfaction as Tiger's spinal cord snapped. Tiger howled like a wild animal, his legs immediately going limp, becoming useless. Forever.

Eli threw the broken Chinese Zodiac Hero to the side with the last of his waning strength. He reached up and tried to pull the knife out of his shoulder, but it was slick with his own blood and he couldn't seem to get a good grip.

Oh well, Eli thought. For some reason it didn't seem like that big a deal. He didn't feel the pain so much, either. It was receding into the distance, unimportant. How much blood had he lost?

Eli heard a thumping sound and tried to raise his head. Rooster was dragging the still screaming Tiger out of his bedroom, muttering in Russian under his breath. The Hero of Aquarius didn't speak Russian, but cursing has a way of crossing language barriers. Eli allowed himself a brief smile.

146

Rapidly shrinking back to his normal size, Eli let his head fall back down to the gray carpet that was now stained an ugly maroon. It didn't matter. Rooster, Tiger, this whole gods damned conflict with the American Zodiac and the Chinese Zodiac. None of it mattered. How come no one else could see that?

Rooster suddenly loomed large above him, one of Tiger's knives held in his good hand.

--*Bro?*-- Edgar's voice slid sideways between his sluggish thoughts, coming from a long way off. Must be in San Francisco with the others. That was good. --*Eli, are you ok? I tried to make contact but something was block--*

--*It's ok*-- Eli cut him off. --*I got Tiger...out of the fight.*--

Rooster knelt down next to him. His face was grim, the face of judgment. He had one of Tiger's knives in his right hand.

--*Are you ok?*-- Edgar's telepathic voice sounded frantic. He must have felt something from Eli's end.

--*Don't come for me.*-- Eli thought back with as much force as he could muster. --*Stay with the others. They need you.*--

Rooster raised the knife.

--*Eli!*-- Edgar's telepathic voice became a scream.

--*Sally was right, bro. We need to be better. If we're not, then what's the point?*--

The knife fell.

--*Love you, bro.*--

Everything went black.

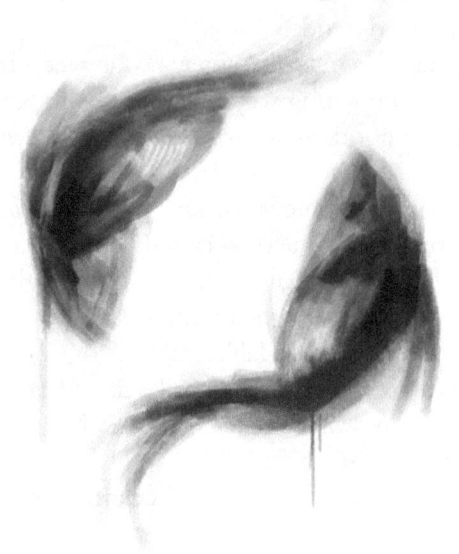

CHAPTER 12

PISCES

Pisces, the 12th and final sign on the Zodiac wheel, is represented by two fish swimming eternally opposite, one white and one black. This symbol represents the dual nature of Pisces. Realistic balanced by mystic. Good balanced by evil. Healer balanced by destroyer. It is said that under Pisces shall all things come to an end.

11:35 PM PST, February 28, 2016

"Are we absolutely sure that we don't want to include Ariele? I mean, she *is* our leader, for the most part," Quinton asked, looking up from the rickety wooden desk that sat in the corner of his modest-sized living room, papers spread out before him. The shorter of the two Pisces Heroes, Quinton stood at just under 6 feet. He was whipcord strong, without a single ounce of body fat on his lean frame. With his light brown hair cut into a stylish hairdo and clean-shaven cheeks emphasizing his high cheekbones and handsome face, he could have easily passed for a GQ model.

Still wracked with guilt over the death of Eli, it had been Quinton's idea to scrap the plan put forth by the other Heroes and strike out on their own. The papers scattered in front of him bore the names and powers of all of the other American Zodiac Heroes.

The two Pisces Heroes had been holed up in Quinton's apartment back in Salt Lake City, Utah since the previous day, refining and rehashing their plan, trying to find every chink in their armor and subsequently figure out a way to fix it or work around it.

Max rubbed his eyes and yawned. The 6'1" shaven headed 23 year old had purple bags under his eyes that showed how sleep deprived he was. Max stretched his thick arms toward the ceiling to try and relieve some of the soreness in his lower back and was rewarded with a loud popping noise as his spine cracked and adjusted. He sighed contentedly. "I just don't see how she can help, man. We need people with strength to help us do what needs to be done."

"Her entire power is based around being able to make sense of the world around her," Quinton pointed out, finger stabbing down on the piece of paper that had all of Ariele's information on it.

"But the place we're going to, from what I understand of it, *defies* sense and logic. I think that instead of Ariele helping, she'd lose her mind instead. I won't have any more casualties on my head," Max

149

countered, eyes drooping. The two Pisces Heroes had been over this again and again, chasing around the same points of contention like a dog chasing its tail.

Quinton sighed and bent down over the papers to study them yet again.

After Eli had given his life while protecting them, the whole team had felt torn apart, none more so than the Pisces Heroes. Eli's older brother Edgar, Hero of Cancer, had vanished without a trace. Coincidentally, they hadn't heard anything from Rooster, either. Even Ivy with her psychic Pull hadn't been able to locate them.

A quick funeral had been thrown together for Eli with the promise that they would do something more significant and meaningful for their fallen teammate after this whole mess had been resolved once and for all.

Assuming, of course, that they *could* win this war.

The plan, as it stood now, was simple: wait. They knew the Dragon god's endgame was to somehow use the inherent power of life and death that the Pisces Heroes tapped into so that the god could break free of this world and find a new one. The power of any Hero was always stronger during their month on the Zodiac wheel, and stronger still on their birthday. Max and Quinton had birthdays two days apart, Quinton's being on March 2 and Max's on March 4. Logically, Ariele reasoned, the Dragon god would attack on March 3, when the pair would be strongest together.

Thanks to the efforts of Sally and Peter (and Eli; never forget Eli's selfless sacrifice) all of the major Chinese Zodiac Heroes had been taken out of the fight. So when the Dragon god came calling, the American Zodiac Heroes would be able to merge all of their respective abilities together, use Brock to balance the battleground, and destroy the Dragon god once and for all.

It was a good plan, and simple. All of the best plans were. But the fact remained that no matter how powerful all of the Heroes were, they were still going up against a god. The risk that some of them would die was monumental. The other Heroes claimed not to care, that the point was not to save themselves but to save the rest of the world, but the Pisces Heroes disagreed. They wouldn't have any more blood on their hands. Max and Quinton meant to strike first, surprise the Dragon god in a way he would never expect.

"Ok, I can see your point about Ariele," Quinton finally conceded, not looking up. His eyes were focused on the page in front of him. "But what about Taurus? You said you want strength, and no one on our team is stronger than Barin."

Max sighed, frustrated. "I thought about him, but the problem there is that he's been dating Karina, and they're close enough now that they've developed an unshakable psychic connection. And we already said, *no psychics*. We just don't know what this place could do to their minds once we get there. The only reason I want to involve Sagittarius is because Peter is the one person who can get us there. And luckily his girlfriend Ivy is the Push Gemini, not the Pull. Fingers crossed she won't know we're planning something until we're already gone."

Quinton crossed off Barin's name, then frowned as he glanced over at the page of information about the Gemini Twins. "Wait a minute, Ivy isn't the Push Gemini, she's the Pull!"

Max hurriedly crossed the living room to look at the Gemini page. There in front of them, in bold letters, the page read:

Ivy. Age 30. Lives: SF, CA. PULL.

Max cursed under his breath. "Well, it's too late to change our plan now. I guess we just have to hope that Peter's mind is so twisted that Ivy won't be able to accidentally glean any info about what we're dragging her boyfriend into."

Quinton finally looked up at his friend and fellow Pisces Hero. "And if she does?"

"We cross that bridge when we come to it. Fact of the matter is, if we don't have Peter, then we don't have a plan. So let's drop the issue for now and move on to the rest of our team. Agreed?"

Quinton nodded wearily and pulled another page in front of his tired eyes. Max went into the kitchen to put on another pot of coffee.

An hour later, the two young demigods had come up with a definitive list of who they wanted to bring:

Peter, Hero of Sagittarius, to provide the gateway.

Brock, Hero of Libra, to open the door for the rest of them.

Madeleine, Hero of Aries, to handle anything they weren't expecting.

Imani, Hero of Scorpio, to generate the darkness.

And lastly, the two Pisces Heroes, to kill a god.

8:00 PM PST, March 1, 2016

"I promise," Max said soothingly to the irate Aries Hero. "we'll explain everything as soon as Peter gets here."

Maddy grumbled something under her breath about the two of them being on the same flight and how ridiculous it was that Peter was late, but she backed off. The war Hero was now sitting cross-legged on the living room floor in dark red leggings and a long burgundy t-shirt with her lynx familiar's head in her lap. The lynx, named Spear, was a little bit bigger than the average German shepherd, and it's purring was a low rumble that could be felt by everyone there.

Brock and Imani had arrived right on Maddy's heels. They'd immediately sequestered themselves in the corner of the Quinton's living room in a couple of folding chairs and were conferring quietly. Brock had an idea of what they were there for, and seemed to approve. Now he was doing his best to get Imani on board, as well. She'd been shaky and nervous ever since last Halloween.

There was a loud knock at the door. *Finally*, Quinton thought as he through his living room into the tiled foyer beyond and opened the front door. Peter strolled in wearing tattered blue jeans, blue flip flops that had seen better days, and a black tank top stretched tight across his chest. Peter's body language was casual, but his eyes darted wildly around the apartment as if trying to see everywhere at once. Quinton was pretty sure he hadn't blinked in over a month. The Pisces Hero would have bet even money that the mad Sagittarian didn't even close his eyes when he slept.

"So," Peter said, eyes finally coming around to Quinton and locking on to him with a burning intensity that made Quinton want to back up a few steps. "we're attacking now, huh? Also, Utah is boring. I've been here less than a day and I'm bored. Also, my flight sucked. Don't want to talk about it. Let's talk about how we're attacking now."

Quinton blinked. "Uh...how did you know?"

Peter snorted. "Oh please, look who you gathered here. Have the six of us ever gotten together outside of a full war meeting? Not to mention your weird secrecy and convincing all of us to jump on a plane to Utah because it's less likely to be on the Dragon god's radar. Don't get me wrong, I like you guys, you all seem like good people, but when you call a madman to a secret meeting and you specifically tell said madman not to invite his psychic girlfriend, obviously something's up. So are we attacking now or not, because I'm in."

Maddy gently pushed her lynx's head out of her lap and climbed to her feet while Imani and Brock broke off their private conference and joined them in the foyer.

Max walked over to stand next to Quinton and crossed his arms over his chest, nodding briskly. "Yes, we're attacking now. Doesn't it bother you to leave Ivy behind?"

"You think I want to endanger her, or anyone else? Whatever your plan is, I'm sure you've already taken into consideration the fact that not all of us are going to come back from this. Hence the smaller team. Which I fully approve of. Enough of us have died already."

Quinton and Max looked around the circle of Heroes as everyone voiced their agreement without hesitation. "So we don't have to convince you to come along?"

Maddy reached down and stroked Spear's furry head. "Just tell us where we're going."

"I don't know if it has a name," Max said slowly, turning back to Peter. "but he's the only one who's been there."

"You can't be serious," Peter said, eyes widening. "*That's* your plan?! You want to take us all to the heart of madness and take on the Dragon god on his home turf?! And you call *me* the crazy one!"

"It's your 'home turf' too!" Quinton snapped irritably. His hands were clenching and unclenching nervously at his side. This had to work! "We're going to use Brock's balancing power to bring us all to *your* level, and then enter that place in the flesh."

"You don't know what you're asking," Peter whispered, eyes bulging out of his head. "not even *I* have ever entered that hellish dimension in the flesh before. I'm connected psychically, but to go there physically? *None* of us may be able to come back from that! Are you all so gung ho to throw your lives away?"

"To save the world?" Imani said in a quivering voice. "Yes." Brock put a comforting hand on her shoulder.

One by one, the rest of them nodded, even the lynx.

Peter giggled softly. "Alright, fuck it. Let's do this." The mad Hero held up a hand, pointing at each of his teammates. "But for safety, if any of you has a transformation to whip out, you should probably do it now. Who knows what you could turn into if you transform *there*."

The group moved back into the living room. Max and Quinton rushed around, pushing a couch and a couple of end tables out of the way to make room for them all to stand in a circle in the center of the room. Posters of various heavy metal bands lined the walls, watching the transpiring events with what seemed to be approval.

Maddy closed her eyes and reached into herself, into the heart of her power. The war spirit within her begged for release. Maddy hesitated for a single moment...and then let it out. Her red leggings and burgundy top rippled, appearing to melt apart and then segment back together as they hardened into overlapping organic-metallic discs the color of blood. The armor was part of her, and would allow for ease of movement while providing full body protection. Her lynx, Spear, stretched and flattened, becoming a 7-foot long spear in truth, topped at either end with a wicked spike. The head of the spear bulged out on either side, hardening into curved, half moon axe blades.

Brock's clothes and skin began to shimmer, lightening to a bright white on one side of his body and darkening to a matte black on the other. Even his eyes changed, one turning white and the other turning black. He had become a human set of scales, balancing light and darkness.

Imani drew in a deep breath, gathering in all of the shadows in the room. Within seconds she appeared to be clothed in pure darkness, flowing and undulating around her. Her eyes were two onyx orbs.

Max and Quinton, as one, reached up to their foreheads, mentally summoning their inner darkness. Masks so black they seemed to pull light in appeared out of nothing on top of their heads, and the two Pisces Heroes grasped hold and yanked them down over their faces. The masks molded to their skin, stretching tight and sinking in, becoming part of them. The young demigods felt their very personalities shifting, becoming as black as their masks. Morality went flying out the window. They became agents of death itself.

Peter watched his teammates transforming around him without saying a word. His own transformation was triggered by stress and adrenaline rather than conscious will, and in truth he had only managed it a small handful of times ever since first getting his power. The last time he'd changed was almost a year ago, when this whole damn thing had started. Peter had transformed when he and

Max and Barin had come to Maddy's rescue. It seemed like a lifetime ago.

Only minutes had passed, and they were all as ready as they'd ever be.

"One last word of advice," Peter offered, voice harsh and unyielding. "No matter what happens when we get there, your true selves will still be within you. Hold onto that as hard as you can. If you lose yourself before we can finish off the Dragon god, then this whole trip may be for nothing." So saying, Peter reached out a hand to Max on one side, and Brock on the other.

One by one, all of the gathered American Zodiac Heroes joined hands, sealing them all together in a circle of power such that the world hadn't seen in generations. Peter turned to Brock. "Ready?"

Brock nodded, closing his eyes. Delving into his power, he envisioned two great glowing hands. One hand reached out into Peter's mind, into the heart of Sagittarius, searching for the gateway to his madness. The other stretched out through the circle behind him, gathering up the essence of his friends and teammates.

The gateway appeared in Brock's mind. It was in the shape of a twisted doorframe, full of angles and sharp edges that tore at his sanity. Behind the doorframe glowed a pulsing orange light, sickening and putrid. Brock wanted nothing more than to throw up, cut the connection to Peter's mind and run away screaming.

Instead, Brock kicked the door open and dragged them all through it, into a place where dreams turned to nightmares, a place that had never known balance since the creation of the universe itself. Brock's mind, unable to comprehend a sheer lack of even a semblance of balance, shut down. He was unconscious before he hit the ground.

The Hero of Libra awoke to the feeling of pain in his cheek. Peter was kneeling over him, face grim, hand upraised for another slap.

The mad Sagittarian reached down and grabbed Brock by the shoulders, leaning his bearded face in close. "You want to survive this place and do what we came here to do?" Peter growled. "Then don't try to look for balance. Here, *you* are the only balance. Hold to that!"

Brock nodded weakly and struggled up to his feet. Standing in a ring around him, facing outwards, were the others. Maddy, spear held slanted across her chest as if facing down a charge of enemies, stared uneasily off into the distance. Max and Quinton stood on either side of her, bodies quivering like drawn bowstrings. Behind him Imani stood guard, watching his back in her gown of shadows. Brock finally got a good look at the place he had taken them all to, and his mind very nearly shut down again.

The place was *vast*, seemingly as big as the known universe. It's sheer size weighed down on him. Flatland stretched out in every direction, randomly throwing out jagged mountain peaks in the distance that looked like the shattered teeth of some demonic beast. Even as he stared, a mountain off to the left near the horizon shattered apart, crumbling down into dust.

And the colors! The flatlands were various shades of putrid orange, looking like some kind of diseased desert. The sky above their heads was a sickly yellow streaked with black. The colors twisted together where the sky met the ground on the horizon, clashing and fragmenting apart. The mountains were peaked with red and black like dormant volcanoes. A frigid wind howled past. Brock thought he could almost hear voices in that wind, gibbering in fear and madness.

Brock reached out and grabbed hold of Peter like a drowning man clutching desperately at a piece of driftwood to keep his head above water. "How can you stand this?" he choked out hoarsely. "How can you stand having part of your mind here and never being able to leave?"

Peter grinned mirthlessly. "We endure what must be endured," he said wryly, shaking his head. "Besides, when part of it is inside of you, it doesn't seem quite so...*alien*."

Brock leaned over and threw up on the rocky ground at his feet.

"Alright boys and girls!" Peter said loudly, clapping his hands like a teacher in front of his students to get their attention. "*Who's ready to take on a god?!*" He pointed a finger at Maddy, looking for all the world like some kind of deranged orchestra conductor. "ARIES!"

Maddy raised her spear over her head, slammed it down into the ground. As the spike tip shattered through the crust of poisoned earth, the ground began to rumble.

Peter spun on his heel and pointed at Imani. "SCORPIO!"

Imani raised her arms. The streaks of black that stretched across the sky began to pulse, growing, sweeping across the world, plunging them into darkness lit by a malevolent orange glow on the horizon.

Peter pointed over his shoulder without turning. "LIBRA!"

Brock reached within himself for the balance he had brought into this demented world. He let that balance flow through him, forced it out of him, pushing away the madness that crept in from every side. That balance served as a beacon fire to any denizens of this place, and would draw them like iron filings to a lodestone. Brock suddenly saw the brilliant logic of what Peter was doing, of what Max and Quinton had done by bringing this select group of Heroes to this place.

Peter pointed both hands out to either side. "PISCES!"

Max and Quinton raised their masked faces to the black sky and *screamed*. The promise of death could be heard in their voices, and even Imani shivered hearing it. That scream grew in volume and intensity, and spread outward across the land.

At last Peter opened himself up to the twisted land around him. He felt his mind tip precariously, on the brink of falling away into complete insanity, from which he would never return. And on that knife's edge, Peter reached within himself for his own transformation.

The Hero of Sagittarius began to grow. Peter's legs split, shredding his tattered jeans as two legs burst and became four. His torso stretched backwards, skin growing thicker and more dense. Four feet hardened into hooves. His hair grew, lengthening into a brilliant mane that raced down his spine. He reared up on his back legs, and when he landed he was a cross between human and animal, a smaller copy of the god who had given him his powers and his madness. Peter the human had become Peter the centaur.

Max and Quinton abruptly cut off their deathscream as they all felt something *immense* soar through the blackness above them. It was a shadow darker than the sky, stretching to either horizon. And it was laughing.

"**Little humans,**" a voice growled out at them from every direction at once. "**You have brought me what I needed. For this, I thank you. For this, I won't kill your friends. You have done a great service to your people.**"

Peter grinned maniacally. "Well Pisces, guess your plan worked. Nicely done." He turned his head, glancing back over his shoulder at Brock who stood there silently clothed half in shadow, half in light. "Libra, you mind balancing this out a little?"

Brock mentally reached out at the Dragon shadow as it turned, coming around for another pass. He grasped hold of the sheer physical size of the Dragon god's power, much like he had done at Halloween, except that this time he was dealing with the god himself and not just a projection. Gritting his teeth, sweat popping out of his forehead, Brock struggled to pull the Dragon god's power down to their level, to balance the battleground one final time.

The overwhelmingly huge outline of the Dragon god in the sky split right down the middle. What remained was a Dragon shadow that now only covered *half* the sky instead of all of it. The other half of the shadow continued splitting, dividing down over and over again until there were hundreds of Dragon shadows that were the size of the American Zodiac Heroes. An *army* of miniature Dragons.

The Dragon god himself, uncaring of his slightly diminished size and power, laughed savagely as he unleashed his army upon them.

"Line up!" Max shouted at his teammates as the hundreds of Dragon shadows flew at them. "This is why we're here! We take the Dragon god down piece by piece until we can finish him once and for all!"

The Dragon shadows flew in close before dropping to the ground, legs forming beneath them as they took on the look of soldiers. These soldiers carried no weapons; they had no need of them, as the Dragon god expected to overwhelm the American Zodiac Heroes with sheer numbers.

The Heroes lined up, Max and Quinton on either end, with Brock hanging back and desperately trying to maintain his balance effect on the fight.

Maddy, Hero of Aries and alive with the spirit of war burning through her, let out a bestial howl of challenge and ran forward to meet the Dragon soldiers. Her spear was a blur as she flipped it in tight circles around her body, flicking it out to take the head off of the lead soldier with the axe blade that tipped the front end, then dropping to her knees and spinning around with the haft held straight out in front of her to sweep the legs out from another three in a row. In a split second she was back up on her feet, slashing and chopping all around her. Dragon soldiers died silently by the scores as Maddy tapped into her true potential. This was what she had been born to do!

Imani dropped forward onto all fours, pulling more and more shadows around her from the sky above, hardening them around her body into the form of a gigantic scorpion. Delicate hands tipped with giant shadow claws reached out, cutting through Dragon soldiers like a scythe cutting through wheat. When a soldier tried to sneak up on her blind side, a massive shadow stinger flicked down faster than the eye could track and punched a gaping hole through his chest, lifting him into the air and sending him flying.

Max and Quinton, black death pulsing through their veins, each leapt into the fray on legs made stronger by the deadly power they embraced, flying twenty feet through the air in opposite directions to engage their enemy in hand to hand combat.

Max landed on top of one unlucky Dragon soldier, bearing him forcibly down to the ground and breaking his neck as they landed with an audible *CRUNCH!* The Pisces Hero rolled with the momentum and popped back up to his feet, reaching out to grab another soldier by the arm. Turning in a tight circle he lifted the soldier and used him as a flail to knock down a ring of enemies around him.

Quinton landed on his feet and shot his hands out to grip the necks of two soldiers within reach. He smiled behind his mask as he tore their throats out, black blood dripping from his fingers. The other Dragon soldiers near him actually hesitated at his brutality before pressing in to close with the Hero of Pisces, now the Hero of death. Quinton met the attack, grinning broadly. Wherever he or Max went, soldiers died messily.

Peter stayed back to guard Brock. A small flood of soldiers managed to get around the other Heroes and, guided by the mind of the Dragon god, sought to end this fight at the source. Peter reached deeper into his power and a shining silver longbow appeared in his hands, glowing arrow already nocked. A full quiver shimmered into reality on his back. Eyes wide and teeth bared, barely hanging onto his humanity, Peter loosed the arrow. It took a Dragon soldier right through the eye. The corpse fell silently, but more soldiers scrambled over it, trampling the body into the ground. Peter reared up, lashing out with his front hooves and caving in the skulls of the two soldiers nearest him. He landed, shooting arrow after arrow at the growing tide of soldiers.

Brock, sweat pouring down his half glowing, half shadowed face, grinned fiercely. It was working! His teammates slaughtered the Dragon soldiers with wanton abandon, taking relatively few hits in return. Brock bore down and increased the pressure of his balance power, forcing the Dragon god to shrink down and commit more and more of his divine body to the fight. Soon the god covered only a quarter of the sky, and he continued to deflate! Eventually his divine power would be depleted enough that they could launch a direct assault and end this war!

As if reading Brock's thoughts, the insane god abruptly changed his attack. All of the Dragon soldiers that had been focused on Max and Quinton on either flank turned their attention to Imani and Maddy. The soldiers pressed in on the war Hero and the giant scorpion, throwing themselves at the demigods, trying to bury them in an avalanche of bodies.

Maddy screamed in defiance and rose to meet the challenge, fully unleashing her power, her own inherent mad fury. She hurled her spear and it transformed back into a lynx, snarling, slashing and biting at anything that got close. Maddy tore off her armored shirtsleeves and mentally molded them into organic-metallic daggers with razor edges. Spinning wildly, Maddy and her lynx destroyed every soldier that came within reach.

Imani held her own at first, hardened shadow claws and stinger flickering out in every direction, stabbing and slicing and cutting, but there were just so many soldiers. Inside of her shadow scorpion, Imani gritted her teeth, trying to push her fear out of her rather than let it overwhelm her.

Brock, psychically connected to the balance of the battlefield and everyone on it, felt when one soldier managed to dive under Imani's claws. The soldier rolled on the ground, and when he popped up he held a rock in his hand. Brock felt the soldier smash the rock into Imani's face, knocking her to the ground. Dazed, Imani's shadow scorpion vanished around her. The soldier knelt down on the youngest American Zodiac Hero, raised his bloody rock, and brought it down on her skull again. And again. And again.

Brock felt her die, alone and surrounded by enemies.

The Hero of Libra opened his mouth to cry out, and suddenly Peter was looming above him, eyes as cold as the grave. "Use it," Peter commanded. One of his rear legs flashed out, catching an advancing Dragon soldier in the face. Bones crunched beneath

Peter's hoof. "Use it! Don't let her die for nothing! You use this and you finish it! We'll weep for the dead when it's over!" The gargantuan centaur wheeled himself around and the deadly rain of arrows started up once more.

Max, ignorant of Imani's death, had joined Maddy in the middle of the battlefield. They fought back to back, her with her daggers and him with his bare hands, while the lynx was a whirlwind of death on the perimeter of the space they had carved out. Each of them was bleeding from a dozen minor cuts on their arms and faces.

Quinton, blood pouring out of a wound on his left shoulder, was racing back to where Peter and Brock still held the high ground, if barely. Peter raised his bow and shot any soldier that tried to take Quinton down from behind in his mad dash.

Brock whispered a quick apology to Imani's spirit and then threw himself back into the fight, redoubling his efforts. The Dragon god was nearly down to their size, and he was creating fewer and fewer soldiers with every passing minute.

Quinton skidded to a halt next to them, breathing heavily. His left arm dangled uselessly by his side. "You saw Imani?" he gasped out.

"Yes," Peter said grimly.

"And the others?"

"Still alive, at least for now," Peter pointed with his bow to where Max and Maddy were fighting. Maddy had turned her lynx back into a spear for extra reach in her attack. Nearly all of the soldiers around them were dead or dying.

"Guys," Brock interrupted. "look!"

The Dragon god had stopped creating more shadow soldiers, at long last committing himself to the fight personally, and he was heading toward them.

Fast.

Quinton swore. "He's going for Max and Maddy. We'll never get there in time!"

"Maybe you won't have to," Brock said, mind racing. "Quinton, give me your hand!" Quinton held out his right hand and Brock grasped it tightly. With that connection, he reached out with his mind and took hold of Quinton's Pisces power, the power of death. "Peter, give me an arrow!" Without asking questions, Peter pulled a glowing arrow from his quiver and passed it over.

Holding Quinton's power in one hand and Peter's in the other, via the arrow, Brock forced a balance between the two, merging them together. Peter's arrow, at first silver and glowing with an inner light, turned as black as Quinton's deathmask. Brock hurriedly handed the arrow back to the centaur.

Peter looked at the transformed arrow in his hand. "You really think this will work?" he asked doubtfully.

"It has to," Brock said. "We'll never get another chance like this. So make it count, for Imani."

"For Eli," Quinton whispered.

The Hero of Sagittarius nocked the arrow and drew it back to his cheek in one fluid motion. "For Andy," he said grimly. The glowing bowstring twanged, and the arrow of death shot out with a hiss.

The Dragon god, now the size of a semi truck and bearing down rapidly on Max and Maddy, flared his body and spread his wings wide, wicked sharp claws outstretched on tree trunk limbs. Max and Maddy planted their feet and readied themselves for a final attack.

The black arrow sailed over the heads of the Heroes with barely a whisper and entered the Dragon god's chest, piercing his twisted heart. The god screamed, and the whole universe shook with the force of it.

"*MADDY! MAX! GET YOUR ASSES OUT OF THERE!*" Peter bellowed at the top of his lungs. The two Heroes turned and sped away as fast as their legs could carry them.

The Dragon god hit the ground in his death throes. With each convulsion, the land around him shook, coming apart at the seams. This place, twisted as it was, couldn't physically bear the dying of a god.

Time seemed to slow down like in a nightmare. Which, Brock conceded to himself, was 100% accurate. Max and Maddy ran as if through molasses as a dying god tore the world apart behind them. Each seizure forced the arrow of death deeper into the Dragon god's heart. Obsidian blood poured out onto the ground under him, sizzling and smoking, eating through the poisoned soil like acid. Distant mountain ranges shattered apart. The ground heaved up as earthquakes shook in time with the Dragon god's death throes.

Peter released his power, shrinking back down to his human form, and gathered his shredded clothes around himself.

Quinton reached up and tore his deathmask off of his face with his good right hand. The shreds of stygian blackness, once pulled away from his face, turned into smoke and vanished. Max did the same as he ran toward his teammates, legs pumping.

Maddy dropped her spear as she ran, and it transformed back into a lynx racing along beside her.

Brock was the only one who held onto his transformation out of necessity. The Hero of Libra reached out and grasped hold of Quinton's dangling left hand, grabbed Peter's right hand. The other two Heroes ran up and completed the circle just as the ground split beneath them.

"*GO!*" Max screamed, voice lost in the whirlwind of destruction around them.

Brock shut his eyes, blocking out everything except his connection to his friends and his connection to his power. Once more the Hero reached out with mental hands, gathering the other Heroes in one hand and finding the doorway back to their world through Peter with the other. Wasting no time, Brock shoved that door open and dragged them all through just as the world of madness collapsed in on itself.

The strain was too much for Brock's mind. His last coherent thought was a prayer offered up for Imani's spirit.

Quinton woke up in a hospital in downtown San Francisco, the hospital that was specially equipped to treat demigods. His body felt like one gigantic bruise, and his left arm was strapped to his chest in a sling. Gauze was wrapped tightly around his shoulder. Quinton's mouth was as dry as a desert, and he felt like he hadn't had anything to drink in ages.

Cracking open eyelids that felt gummed shut, the Pisces Hero looked around the room he was lying in. It was a big room, white, sterile, exactly what he had expected. Brock was in the bed on his left, unconscious and plugged into an IV bag that was dripping a clear fluid into his arm. A monitor on his bedside table was beeping periodically.

Feeling a pinch in his right arm, Quinton noticed that he, too, was plugged into an IV. His head felt stuffed full of wool, and he had to fight down the urge to yank that IV out, because that's what they always did in the movies.

The door opened and Max peeked into the room. Seeing Quinton awake, the other Hero of Pisces tiptoed in, shutting the door quietly behind him so as not to bother Brock. Max looked like Quinton felt, black and blue from head to toe. Numerous small bandages covered Max's arms and face.

"You're up!" Max exclaimed as quietly as he could, rushing over and dropping into the chair next to Quinton's bed, a broad smile lighting up his face.

Quinton nodded his head in Brock's direction. "Is he...?" he croaked out.

"He's fine. Or at least, he will be. The doctor said that he suffered a mini stroke or something. Must have been the strain of getting us all out of there in one piece."

Quinton let out a breath that he hadn't realized he'd been holding. "Thank the gods for that. How's everyone else?"

The smile on Max's face slipped and fell. "Imani didn't make it. The Dragon god got her before we got him. But we *did* get him, for her sake and for everyone else! We won!" Max said fiercely, fire burning in his eyes.

Just like that, Quinton remembered everything. Fighting alone, trying to get closer to the giant shadow scorpion that was his teammate. Seeing a Dragon soldier slip under her defenses. Watching helplessly as the soldier raised a rock and slammed it down...Quinton shook his head angrily, and a tear slid down one cheek. The electronic monitor near his bed began beeping.

Max got back up to his feet. "I'll give you some time," he told his friend gently. "When you're ready, the rest of us are here. They weren't even mad that we went off on our own like we did. Well, they were a little mad at first, but they're mostly just happy that it's over. And it *is* over. We did it, buddy." Max patted Quinton on his good arm before turning and walking out of the room.

Quinton lay there in his hospital bed, staring up at the ceiling. He thought about the past year, about everything that had happened. He thought about what it meant to be a superhero. He thought about the self-sacrifice, about putting yourself on the front lines over and over again to protect a world full of people he had never even met. He thought about Andy, and Eli, and Imani. He thought about himself, and how he would feel if it had been him to give up his life

164

to bring this war to an end, stopping a mad god bent on tearing the world apart in his quest to find a new one.

Finally, hours later, Quinton came to a decision. Being a superhero, giving yourself to something more, even if it meant giving your life for the sake of the world itself, was worth it. If his time came, he wouldn't run from the moment, he would embrace it. Because it wasn't about him, in the end. It was about everyone else. His Zodiac offered themselves up in sacrifice so no one else would have to.

Max poked his head in a little later to see if Quinton was ready to talk to everyone. He saw his friend lying asleep in his hospital bed, a content smile on his face. Max softly closed the door without waking him. After all, there was no rush. Not anymore. The war was over.

THE END...

EPILOGUE

Excerpt from the diary of Max, Hero of Pisces

3/2/16
We won. Enough said.

3/2/16
It's my birthday. Despite this whole war being over,
I'm not feeling like partying. There's something that
keeps bothering me.

Let me back up. Earlier today I was released from the
hospital. First thing I did was go over to Peter's
place. Asked him to call Ivy and get her over, too. I
explained to the two of them that I wanted to make
sure this thing really was over. I asked Ivy to use
her Pull on the entire Chinese Zodiac roster around
the world.
She did.
Nearly every one of their Heroes was accounted for
and deemed a non-threat, including Sheep, who, it
turns out, lives in Vietnam and is a pacifist. I don't
understand that, considering the nature of how the
Chinese Zodiac Heroes get their powers, but
whatever. All I care about is that they aren't secretly
still plotting against us.
There was only one Hero that Ivy couldn't locate,
and it's been plaguing me ever since I left Peter's
house.

Who and where the hell is Boar???

INDEX OF

CHARACTERS

AMERICAN ZODIAC HEROES

ARIES

March 21 - April 20

Name: Maddy
Age: 22
Lives: San Francisco, CA.
Attributes: 5'10", Caucasian, red hair, slender2
Animal familiar: Lynx with a partly magical soul, possesses the ability to transform into a living spear.
Powers: Enhanced strength, speed, and endurance. Can mentally transform any clothing into her battle attire. Soul imbued with the essence of war.

TAURUS

April 21 - May 21

Name: Barin
Age: 31
Lives: San Francisco, CA
Attributes: 6'0", Pakistani-American, black hair, stocky
Powers: Wildly enhanced strength. Can turn skin to organic stone. When in stone form, becomes immovable to any force. Can also erect psychic stone barriers around his mind as a mental defense.

GEMINI

May 22 - June 21

Name: Ivy
Age: 30
Lives: San Francisco, CA
Attributes: 5'3", Caucasian, auburn hair, slim
Powers: Can Pull anything, mental or physical

Name: Karina
Age: 32
Lives: San Francisco, CA
Attributes: 5'4", Argentine-American, black hair, curvy
Powers: Can Push anything, mental or physical

Additional note on Gemini 'Twins': Can meld minds and use Push/Pull simultaneously. If one Hero is rendered unconscious, the other Hero can wield both Push and Pull.

CANCER

June 22 - July 22

Name: Edgar
Age: 34
Lives: Chicago, IL.
Attributes: 5'10", Israeli-American, dark brown hair, compact and muscular, older brother of Aquarius Hero (Eli)

Name: Alex
Age: 37
Lives: New Orleans, LA
Attributes: 6'3", Scottish-American, light brown hair, heavily muscled

Powers: Sideways shifting (nearly teleporting), sideways telepathy

LEO

July 23 - August 22

Name: Andy
Age: 34
Lives: San Francisco, CA
Attributes: 5'10", Caucasian, light brown hair, portly but strong
Powers: Sun heart, plasma energy in veins instead of blood, allows him to instantly cauterize and wounds, extendable burning claws, short burst super speed, extendable fangs

VIRGO

August 23 - September 23

Name: Ariele
Age: 30
Lives: Jackson Hole, WY
Attributes: 6'0", Canadian-American, dirty blonde hair, slender
Powers: Auto analysis (can look at a person or situation and instantly understand everything about it), 360 degree perspective (mental awareness of everything around her), Command voice (force others to obey)

LIBRA

September 24 - October 23

Name: Brock
Age: 31
Lives: Salt Lake City, UT
Attributes: 5'8", Caucasian, blond hair, stocky
Powers: Balance power (can bring another person to his level, or bring himself to another persons level).

SCORPIO

October 24 - November 22

Name: Imani
Age: 18
Lives: Salt Lake City, UT
Attributes: 5'6", Somali-American, brown hair, skinny
Powers: Darkness manipulation which can be enhanced by fear, enhanced healing

SAGITTARIUS

November 23 - December 21

Name: Peter
Age: 30
Lives: San Francisco, CA
Attributes: 6'1", Caucasian, brown hair, muscular, mentally unbalanced to an unknown degree
Powers: Never misses anything thrown or shot, can transform into a centaur when under severe stress

CAPRICORN

December 22 - January 20

Name: Sally
Age 29
Lives: Salt Lake City, UT
Attributes: 5'5", Caucasian, dirty blonde hair, slender
Powers: Can climb anything with the slightest edge to it, can phase through solid objects as if they were made of water. Can split her body in two while still being connected by one mind and use both powers simultaneously.

AQUARIUS

January 21 - February 19

Name: Eli
Age: 30
Lives: New York City, NY
Attributes: 6'1", Israeli-American, brown hair, thickly muscled, younger brother of Cancer Hero (Edgar)
Powers: 'Better vibe', can be used outwardly to make the world around him better, or inwardly to make himself better, genius intellect

PISCES

February 20 - March 20

Name: Quinton
Age: 23
Lives: Salt Lake City, UT
Attributes: 5'9", Caucasian, dark blond hair, slim and athletic

Name: Max
Age: 23
Lives: Salt Lake City, UT
Attributes: 6'0", Caucasian, shaved head, muscular

Powers: 'Light' ability: enhanced charisma, enhanced acrobatic agility.
'Dark' ability: can manifest a mask of darkness (deathmask), enhanced
speed, enhanced strength

CHINESE ZODIAC HEROES

RAT

Male
Age: Between 30 and 40
Attributes: 5'4", Caucasian, emaciated, black hair, one black eye and one blue eye, cannibal
Powers: Extendable claws, can teleport through shadows

OX

Male
Age: Unknown
Attributes: 6'11", Nigerian, shaved head, incredibly muscular
Powers: Unstoppable force, body is five times the density of a normal human body

TIGER

Male
Age: Between 40 and 50
Attributes: 6'6", British, blonde hair, muscular
Powers: Naturally camouflaging skin allows him to blend in with any surroundings, night vision like his namesake, enhanced speed and strength

RABBIT

Male
Age: Between 30 and 40
Attributes: 6'0", French, brown hair, wiry
Powers: Superhuman jump (has shown the ability to jump across oceans), mental GPS

DRAGON

Male
Age: Between 30 and 40
Attributes: 5'10", British, brown hair, compact
Powers: Dragon transformation, acid blood, fire breathing

SNAKE

Male
Age: Between 40 and 50
Attributes: 5'9", Indian, brown hair, skinny
Powers: Segmented bone structure like his namesake, extendable fangs, poisonous bite

HORSE

Female
Age: 70
Attributes: 5'1", Aboriginal Australian, black hair, scrawny
Powers: Clairvoyant (extent unknown), healer

SHEEP

Female
Age: Unknown
Attributes: 5'2", Vietnamese, black hair, skinny
Powers: Unknown

MONKEY

Male
Age: Unknown due to powers
Attributes: 5'8", Arabian, black hair, skinny
Powers: Shapeshifter, enhanced speed

ROOSTER

Male
Age: Between 40 and 50
Attributes: 6'1", Russian, brown hair, thickly muscled
Powers: Never tires, doesn't need to sleep, brain like a super computer

DOG

Male
Age: Unknown
Attributes: 5'0", Chinese, black hair, thin
Powers: Can look through history, limited clairvoyance, exists within the time stream itself

BOAR

Gender: Unknown
Age: Unknown
Attributes: Unknown
Powers: Unknown